WICKED SUN

VAMPIRES & VICES NO. 3

NINA WALKER

This one is for all those brave souls battling chronic illness, seen and unseen. You are not alone.

CHAPTER 1

ADRIAN

I'm halfway back to Versailles when the royal blood bond breaks. It stops me in my tracks, a chasing wave of unbridled relief and incredible loss. I don't have to see it to know that it's happened--my maker is dead. I press against the nearest building and breathe in deep. It's a learned behavior from a mortality long since abandoned, but right now, *I need to breathe.*

I drop my head low between my knees and try to rid myself of unwelcome emotions. The stone at my back is winter-cold, the night smells of ice and dirt and city. It's everything I can do to keep upright when a bulbous Frenchman appears next to me, inquiring as to why I'm here. A demanding finger taps me on the shoulder. He smells of flour and booze. He's either a concerned citizen or an angry bakery owner or both, but he's most assuredly a fool. Does he not see who I am--what I am?

I can't deal with humans right now. I can't. *"Laisse-*

moi tranquille," I snap, growling at him as my fangs spring from my gums.

The man freezes, eyes going wide and glossy. So glossy I see the monster reflecting back. I'm primed to kill. And I could.

I could--what a revelation.

Brisa is really gone. I have no master, nobody to tell me no, and it's enough to ruin me. His blood smells delicious, but not as good as his fear--that scent is intoxicating. It's the middle of the night in a back alley in Paris. Nobody would see. Nobody would know it was me. What consequences would I have? None.

I want to lunge for him, but I hesitate, and it's enough of a break for him to run. Bad idea. The predatory urge to chase prey rears its ugly head, and I almost do. "No," I demand of myself aloud. "You're stronger than this."

He runs, and I don't follow because that's not who I am anymore. Or maybe it is, maybe it always will be, but it's not who I *want* to be, who I *can* be. There was a time when killing an innocent for sport was natural, but it's been ages since that game, and I've grown to pride myself on my restraint. I don't have a choice in what I am, but I can choose who I am, and I'm not a murderer anymore.

Just because I'm a predator let free from my cage doesn't mean I'm going back to that. I can't say the same for my kind. Whoever that Frenchman is, I hope he sounds the alarm. Humans need to be on high alert.

Gathering myself together, I continue on foot back to Versailles. I'm a blur of motion that the human eye can't catch. Speed allows me to think while running from undesirable emotions. I've always been good at multitasking like that. But I'm angry––that hasn't left me yet, and I'm not sure if I even want it to. "I warned you!" I yell out to a Brisa who no longer exists. "I warned you this would happen, and now you're not here to clean up the mess you've made!"

For as much as I hated Brisa, I hadn't wanted her dead. Not yet, anyway. Not when it would unleash so many of her children to feed as they please and undo decades of hard work. No amount of immortality will make up for the dark shadows we must hide in during the daylight, but having the freedom to live among society and build a life for ourselves has been more than I ever thought possible. In the years since we came out of hiding, I've been happier than I've ever been since becoming a vampire. And for what? For it all to be undone because Brisa wanted a hybrid child? Something she herself had expressly forbidden others from doing?

She of all people should've avoided the risk. Avoiding risk is what allowed her to keep her crown as long as she did. When I'd left for France, I'd expected Evangeline to be my prodigy. I should've seen this coming––Brisa never was good at sharing.

Then again, neither am I.

I scale the palace wall and levitate across the gardens. Not many vampires can fly, so most won't think to look up. I need to get a feel for what I'm dealing with here, a plan before I reveal myself. I don't have children now that Kelli is gone, so there's nobody to sense if I'm still alive or not. I could use this opportunity to slip away, but that's the last thing I want. Even though the New Orleans coven I lead isn't mine through a blood bond, they're still my family, and I will protect them with my life. I hate that I'm not there right now. They need me. Many will be wayward and will get themselves killed.

I expect chaos at the palace. What I don't expect? Stillness. Quiet. Utter Silence.

Where is everyone? Most of the court hadn't been invited to the ritual tonight, only the most select were ushered along to spectate. And of those, surely they didn't all die. They should've scattered when Brisa died but, like me, they would've come back here to see their children and send word to their covens back home. And maybe even to fight for Brisa's place, though it will never be what it was.

Nobody could ever truly replace Brisa, and that had been her true power, and why I'd never found a way to kill her. Oh, I had wanted to try, had dreamed about finding a work around for the blood bond, had fantasized watching her burn . . . but I'm logical. Her death means disaster for my kind.

I enter through an open window on the third floor to a sparse empty bedroom that must belong to one of the human servants. I find her immediately, hearing her thudding heartbeat before I see her. A middle-aged stick of a woman is squashed into the corner, her eyes hollow and her mouth pinched.

"Are you okay?" I ask, first in French and then in English.

She blinks up at me through round fearful eyes. She's lost whatever compulsion Brisa had put over her. I'm surprised she's still here and hasn't run off by now. She starts begging for her life in gasping French--she's still here because she's hiding from the vampires in the palace.

"I'm not going to hurt you," I say in her native French. "You're safe with me."

She nods, but I can sense she doesn't believe me because her heart rate speeds. Tears break from her eyes to stream down her cheeks. "The others . . ." Horror corrupts her tone, and I don't need to ask for clarification.

I already know.

When the royal blood bond broke, any humans in close proximity to the vampires here were likely sucked dry. I don't have time to deal with this, but I'm not going to leave her to be slaughtered either. I gather the tiny woman into my arms and fly her back out to the street. If I can do one good thing tonight, then let this be it. Why should she have to die? I don't compel humans to be my servants like Brisa did. I pay them well. I've built a business I can be proud of, lead a coven I love, have a home I want to keep.

Merde . . . I like my life, enough to compel this human

to slow the news of what happened tonight from spreading. But what difference will it make? Brisa's bond lorded over all of us, and now that's gone. Many coven leaders will continue to enforce our customs, but not all. Some will use this opportunity for blood, and if it gets out of hand, vampires will be forced back into our holes.

Like where Eva is right now.

Thinking of her sends a frenzy of worry through me coupled with an aching need and a hollow fear that I can't will away. I had this stupid idea that she and I could make it work somehow, that I could be with her, really be with her. But that was foolish. She'll never forgive me. Why would she? I wouldn't forgive me.

It was self-preservation, a skill I picked up long ago. When I learned to conceal my emotions, tucking them away to gather dust. When I made Brisa love me. And when I left Eva in the catacombs to face our common oppressor without me.

Damned self-preservation.

No vampire lives as long as I have without being a selfish prick. I had to leave her, I couldn't risk staying. But there's just one problem––what starts as self-preservation can quickly become self-sabotage, and that shit gets old. And lonely. There, I said it. *Lonely. Lonely. Lonely.* I didn't realize how bad it had gotten until I met her.

Eva is my own personal sun. I've found her warmth, and I love it.

And I hate it.

But what if she refuses me? What if I have to feel this aliveness all on my own? Every pain, every hope, every emotion that I've locked away for centuries is now staring me in the face without a way out. She's the only way out. She's it.

The sun.

I have half a mind to forget Versailles and get her out of the catacombs this very second. And I will, as soon as I know what I'm dealing with, what *we're* dealing with. She has three days before she'll turn, but I'll intercept her before that happens. I'll keep her safe. And then I'll kiss her and hold her, and she won't turn into a monster like I am. She'll be wholly herself, and she'll forgive me, and maybe she'll love me, but even if she doesn't love me I'll be content just to have her.

I drop the trembling woman off with instructions to hide and then rush back to the palace. This time, though, it's not quiet. Not even close.

CHAPTER 2

The wind twists my hair back as the car zips down the two-lane highway. My fingers dance on the torrents of air––up down, up down––until the rattling fear in my chest loosens. Even though I'm one step closer to freedom, I'm beginning to question if freedom really exists. It's a strange resignation that my life isn't what I thought it was. It's not like I have lived wearing rose-colored glasses, but things have turned out to be crueler than I imagined.

"You're not planning something stupid are you?" Tate asks, his weathered eyes twinkling with observation. Sometimes it feels like he sees far more than he lets on. It's unsettling in the best of times and terrifying in the others.

When I left Paris this morning, part of me imagined I'd be free, but I know deep down that was wishful thinking. I've traded one prison for another, but escaping an eternity as a vampire is worth whatever Tate has in store for me. It has to be. I'm at his mercy––a man who has manipulated me and lied to my friends, who hid his true identity for his own gains.

I could make him squirm a little with my answer, but I decide to go with the truth because lies feel like quicksand right now. "Nope, even though I want to run away, I won't. I have literally no plans, nowhere to go, and am counting on you not to screw me over."

"You don't like losing control," he prods. "Can't say I blame you. I don't like it either."

My mind flits to Ayla and how she'd say wanting to keep control was a trait of being born in September. I miss her weird zodiac ramblings so much and don't know if I'll ever get to make things right between us. "Yeah, that control freak thing is a problem. That, and I can't stop thinking about the freedom I'll never get to have."

"Ah, freedom." He nods as if he understands how I feel, but I'm the one being held hostage in this situation, not him. "It's such an American concept, you know. In other countries, people care more for unity and the collective good than for individual freedom."

"Well, you have an American accent, so are you saying you're not the same way?" I fight to roll my eyes.

"I was born in Spain, spent many years in Italy, but I've lived all over since I was a small boy." He smiles ruefully. "I guess that makes me a citizen of the world." Sounds pretentious. "I spent most of my formative years in New York City, but I do think I've held onto my sense of community over individual expression."

"So you're a rule follower?" I raise an eyebrow.

He doesn't answer that, and I let it go, trying to relax into the leather seat. It's cool enough that my skin doesn't stick to the upholstery and late enough in the day that I'm starting to grow chilly with the convertible top down. I don't ask him to put it up, though, because I don't mind the cold. It's actually quite refreshing. I breathe it in as if this is the natural state my body prefers. I don't let myself think about it for too long because enjoying the cold isn't my norm. It's actually another thing to add to my freak-out list. Vampires love the cold because they *are* cold, but I'm not going to turn. I refuse.

"Well, I used to think that freedom existed in my own mind," I explain, deciding this conversation with Tate is the best way I'm going to process my emotions. "That no matter what happens to me, I'd be able to control my thoughts and feelings, and that nobody can take that away from me."

"And do you still believe that?" A ray of sunlight glints off his sunglasses as he turns to study me.

A knot forms in my throat, and I shake my head. "I wish I did, but I've come to realize that our thoughts are biased. We see what we want to see, believe what we want to believe, and feel what we want to feel. Sometimes those things keep us more trapped than anything else ever could."

Because even when all the evidence pointed to the contrary, I still allowed myself to fall for Adrian. Not even fall, *I jumped*. And I wanted to believe I was making the right choices with him, that he'd protect me, that he was falling too . . .

I was wrong.

"Ah, now you're catching on," Tate replies.

There's a smugness to his tone that makes me want to punch the smirk off his face. Normally I'd say something snarky. I could point out that he uses young and impressionable human hunters for his dirty work, but I don't. It's not a good idea to poke the bear, and it's not really what's bothering me right now anyway . . .

The truth is, I fell in love with a cold-blooded vampire. I trusted Adrian. I gave myself over to him, offered my heart and my body. And where did it get me? Betrayed. Heartbroken. And worst of all––infected.

Gah! Why can't I get him out of my mind?

Tate has the forethought not to comment further, and we continue on in silence for the next hour. He's been driving all day, and we've only stopped once to go to the bathroom and pick up snacks. We're in a hurry to get to our destination, and as the sun sinks into the horizon, my heart rate accelerates. It would be so easy for me to give in, to go underground and let the venom take control, snuffing out my mortality like a flame starved of oxygen.

I can picture the venom spreading through my body––my olive skin going waxy, my warm muscles hardening like concrete, my limbs growing cold, and fangs bursting through pliable gums. Presumably, I'd become far more beautiful than I am right now, every imperfection smoothed over like a glossy varnish, but I have a hard time imagining that part to be worth it. Human mortality is something so many vamp wannabes would give up at the chance to be powerful and gorgeous. Not me. I can only focus on the bloodthirsty monster that would lurk underneath the false exterior, and it makes me want to scream and cry and hurl myself from Tate's speeding car.

I shake my horrible thoughts away and turn on him. "Where are we going?" I ask for what is probably the hundredth time. The man hasn't given me a straight answer.

"I told you, it's safest for everyone if you trust me to handle this."

Here we go, another man asking me to trust him. "Trusting you got me into this car, didn't it?"

"No, necessity did."

Okay, he has a point. "But why can't I know where we're going? Unless it's somewhere you know I won't agree with, and that's the true reason you won't tell me."

He sighs heavily, as if I'm such a burden when he was the one who sought me out. "You're going to have vampires on your tail for a while. I'm taking you to safety, and I'd rather not disclose the location until we get there."

"Why, though?"

"Because I have more than just you to protect."

"Pardon me if I have a hard time believing you. You haven't been totally honest."

He doesn't respond, and neither do I because I don't have a lot of options––and we both know that.

The man got me out of Paris, and I'm not sure I would've been able to do that on my own. I do know that we're somewhere in the Italian countryside because we had to go through customs between the neighboring countries. I don't have a passport, but the Italian border control officers waved us through without stopping us. My heart had been a riot in my chest, visions of getting stuck in France dancing through my mind, but they must have recognized Tate's vehicle. The vampires are powerful, but whatever Tate is? He's powerful too.

Rolling hills and sweeping vineyards pass by us in a stunning blur of greens, oranges, and every color of beige that Ayla could have easily named. Autumn has come to Italy, and it suits the country well, casting the landscape in a dusty gold and adding texture. The countryside is dotted with little old farmhouses and small towns. I can easily imagine what it must have been like to live in a place like this a few hundred years ago.

We stick to the back roads, never getting near any big cities, which takes us longer to get to wherever we're going. I would normally love this road trip––it's the kind of thing I used to dream about––but it's hard to enjoy with all the questions floating around in my brain and Brisa's venom heating my veins. I'm anxious, and I don't know what's going to happen to me. Is Brisa dead? Did I kill her? Where's Adrian? What about the other vampires, did I kill some of them too?

What if . . . what if . . . what if . . .

I don't have to wonder about our destination for too much longer because an hour later, just as the sun begins its descent and lights up the sky like a fireball behind the mountains, we turn off the two-lane highway and roll into a quaint village. Tate navigates the cobbled streets with familiarity, approaching the edge of town where a gorgeous limestone castle rests on a cliff's edge. Yellowing ivy crawls up one side, and a vast lake twinkles gold and blue at the base of the cliff. The tallest mountains I've ever seen in person tower like ancient giants beyond the lake. These are the kind of mountains that have seen civilizations rise and fall.

"Waiting wasn't so bad, was it?" Tate asks, pulling me from my thoughts.

"Feels like a power play if you ask me," I reply honestly.

He frowns at that. "I'm sorry you feel that way, Eva, but again, I had to be certain we'd make it here in one piece. What if someone intercepted you? God forbid you'd tell them where I was heading."

I fold my arms in on myself, hating that he's right.

"Switzerland is on the other side of these mountains," he points out.

"Well, I'll be honest, I don't know much about northern Italy, though, it is beautiful. Whenever I think of Italy, I think of Rome and Venice and places I've seen touristy photos of." There's a whole wide world out there that I haven't gotten to explore, and I'm suddenly filled with the desire to see it all.

"We own this castle. It's a historical landmark," Tate continues, voice dripping with pride. "My family has more real estate in Italy than any other country in the world, though we do have holdings all over the globe. Rest assured, Evangeline, you're safe with us."

Safe with you as long as I do what you want . . .

"And who is this 'us' that you're referring to?" When he doesn't answer right away I add, "You know I have to ask. You'd be asking the same things if you were in my shoes."

His fingers tighten on the steering wheel for a second and then relax. "All of your questions will be answered when you are ready for the answers."

That's his response? Is he serious right now? But he smiles at me like he's the most trustworthy dude on the planet, and my spidey senses kick in. "You're trying to do your voice manipulation trick," I scoff. "It won't work on me anymore."

Even without my feather talisman, I have no trouble blocking the manipulation. Must be the venom. His jaw tightens. Maybe I shouldn't have said anything. "I figured as much."

"Listen, I'm not sure how much time we have together for you to answer these questions," I point out. "What if the vamps get to me before you can tell me the things I need to know? You were the one who warned me that I'll have vampires after me for the rest of my life."

"Hmm . . . I did say that, didn't I?"

Not only do I want to know what Tate is, but I wanna know what I am as well because I'm starting to suspect that we might have a few things in common. It's scary to even consider it, and I can't know for sure, but Brisa's words keep ringing in my head about how I'm "both." She acted as if I would've been a valuable piece on her chessboard, knocking courtesans and even princes out of my way.

Looking at my hands, I remember how they'd glowed. Why had they done that? What did it mean? They're completely fine now, just small hands with long fingers and shiny black nail polish. From the outside, I look like a typical nineteen-year-old girl, but I know that can't be true. I gaze up at the approaching castle and sigh. The fortress is intimidating, and Tate's people can't be trustworthy, but hopefully, I'll find answers here.

CHAPTER 3

The castle has a tall outer wall with only one arched opening visible. We pass through it, and I note the guards with semi-automatic weapons who wave us on by. These types of weapons used to be illegal in most of the world, but ever since the vampires came out of hiding, gun laws stopped being enforced. I can't say I blame people for wanting to pack heat, but the sight of guns makes me nervous. Hopefully, they're here to keep me safe, but I kind of doubt they can stop a determined vampire. Fangers are much stronger than bullets, and even the silver ones only slow them down.

We wind up a thin cobblestone drive lined with olive trees that have lost most of their leaves this late in the season. The fallen leaves crunch under our tires like scraps of paper bags. We approach the castle, and I frown at a large gravel parking lot off to one side. Tourists climb onto buses and several of them stop to gawk at us as we round the corner. I end up gawking right back. This is so weird.

"So do I get an official tour?" I ask, only halfway sarcastically because, even though I'm surprised to see tourists, I actually am curious to explore the castle. I never got to explore Versailles, which is a shame.

"Tomorrow," he replies, bullish, and a little smile greets my lips.

We continue to the backside of the castle and pull into an automatic garage. It's a surreal reminder of my arrival to Versailles. A chill zips through my body——I'd rather forget that place ever happened, impossible as that is. Every time I close my eyes, I see the gilded palace and the garish parties and Queen Brisa and her raucous court of nightmares. And then it's Adrian's face that's behind my eyelids, and it's his calloused hands on my body, and those possessive kisses staining my lips . . . and then I *remember*.

"Are you locking me up in here like some kind of princess?" I think of those huge guns and wonder if they're not to keep people out but to keep people in.

Tate doesn't answer as the garage door closes behind us, which sets me on edge. We climb out of the car, and I shake out my sore limbs, then follow Tate to a thick metal door similar to the one back in the hunter's gym. The vampires were all about security too, which I've learned to appreciate only when I'm on the receiving side of security.

"If vampires can't enter a building without being invited in," I question. "Why so much security?"

Tate looks at me sidelong. "Did you learn nothing under my tutelage?"

He's right. It's a silly question. Vampires always find ways to get what they want.

"This is private property, but it's not a proper home. It hasn't been for so many generations that even if we tried to make it one now, it wouldn't stop the vampires." He gives me a level-headed look. "You learned this during your studies. I distinctly remember the lesson. Besides that, vampires get into the homes they really want to get into. There's always someone they can compel."

I hold up my hands in surrender, and my mind floods with the faces of the friends I made while training to become a hunter. They must hate me by now. They came all the way to France to save my ass only to find me playing house with the enemy. They wanted me to go with them, they came to save me, and I'd refused to leave Versailles. If they find me now, no doubt they'll kill me. Would I even blame them? It's what I would've done once upon a time. I never thought I would have allowed Adrian to get to me as he did. I just hope my friends are okay--that Felix and Ayla are doing well and that Seth has found a better team member to boss around. I was never any good at being a team player.

My thoughts move to Kenton, and my heart breaks

all over again. Why do the brightest souls have to be the ones here for the shortest time? It's not fair. He deserved so much better. He had his whole life ahead of him——a family who loved him, a promising talent for lacrosse, and a few years away from finishing an engineering degree at a prestigious university. His laugh was infectious, he was so kind, wicked smart, and made everyone happier. My eyes fill with held-back tears. I'll mourn him when I have a moment alone, but right now I don't want to cry in front of anyone.

And I hate that I can't be vulnerable, that I can't cry, that I can't be myself. Then again, I don't even know who I am anymore.

"We like to keep things authentic for the tourists. It's all part of our cover. Hiding in plain sight, you see? But rest assured, there are many parts of this castle that are renovated with modern conveniences and stay off-limits to the outside world," Tate says as we approach a set of stairs. I wonder what he thinks of losing Kenton and if he even cares. He's lost hunters before and will lose them again. The man purposely puts them in harm's way. "You'll be safe here, and that's what matters."

His words directly oppose my thoughts, and I snort. "Safe somewhere that is open to tourists? Because I've seen enough movies to know that people have ways around guards and locks, and here you are letting them get in the building."

"Don't believe everything you see in films." He chuckles condescendingly, and I fight off the urge to slap him. "Only part of the castle is for tourists and only during the daylight hours."

"Vampires have loyal humans working for them, humans who could have come here today. You know that."

"Yes, but I also know how the vampires think. They'll be looking for you somewhere much more remote. They won't think to track you to a public landmark. And if they do, we have plenty of guards, security cameras, silver bars on all the windows, weapons . . ." His voice trails off when he sees the worried look on my face. "Come along, we need to keep moving."

We climb stairs with no railings, and I pray I don't fall. They're incredibly narrow, and twist up steeply like the turret staircases in medieval films. I can almost see myself carrying an oil lamp while dressed in a sweeping gown, rushing off to solve a mystery or meet a lover. My sorry calves burn with the effort, but I don't complain because the higher we climb, the less anxious I feel. It's like being lifted from a trance or waking up from a too-long nap. My thoughts become clearer, and I feel more like myself. But part of me––a tiny part that surely belongs to Brisa's venom––wants to go back and dig myself a grave in the nearest graveyard, to make the earth my bed and the soil my blanket. I'm ridiculously tired, and I could sleep one last time and wake up with a new life, one without human restraints.

"Right this way," Tate cuts into my thoughts, and I snap out of it. He directs me to a tiny room, but I can hardly pay attention, I'm so bothered by the daydream. No, not just a daydream, it was a fantasy of being a vampire. Why would I think that? I hate vampires. I can't let myself go there ever again, and yet it's something that's been happening in the back of my mind on and off all day.

"Everything you need is already here."

I step inside and blink, trying to take it in and clear my mind. The room is sparse. There's a fluffy full-sized bed with a white duvet blanket on the far wall with a stack of pillows, a square window opposite with a view of the lake and the alps beyond, and . . . that's it.

"I don't need much, but a toilet would be nice," I say dryly.

He points to the corner where a wooden bucket sits next to a roll of toilet paper. I blink, confused and then horrified. "Sure, I can picture myself in another century here, but I wouldn't go so far as this."

"Forgive me, Eva. But this room is the safest we could outfit for you on such short notice. We need to make sure you're locked up tight and above ground tonight."

I turn on him and glare. "Excuse me?"

"It's for your own good," he says, and then he's backing through the doorway, the lock clicking into place.

CHAPTER 4

My first instinct is to panic, but I force myself to stay calm. Terror grips my mind. How far am I willing to go to do the right thing?

Maybe Tate has it right--minutes ago I was fantasizing about finding a graveyard and finishing where Brisa left off. If locking me up in here means that I don't do something crazy, then so be it. But couldn't they have at least given me a television or a book?

I wander over to the window and brace myself against the glass, watching the last of the sunset fade away. As Tate said, there are thick silver bars crossing over the glass, but I try not to think too much about those--I'm not allergic to them, but they remind me of what I've come so close to becoming.

The sunset reflects off the water in a sea of melted honey. I've never met a sunset I didn't like, but this one is proving otherwise because as the sun slides behind the horizon, my body starts to buzz again. I groan and clutch my arms to my chest, trying not to scratch what feels like angry ants burrowing into my skin.

A familiar pain shoots through my head--the beginning of a migraine.

I squint and hurry to the bed to sprawl out on top of the duvet. I don't want to climb inside the fluff because it's way too hot up here. It wasn't so hot when I arrived a few minutes ago, but now it's like I've been trapped in a sauna. Could Tate have turned on a heater? Sweat begins to bead along my forehead.

"This is just the venom," I whisper, trying to reason this out, to talk myself down from letting the ball of panic in my chest explode and send shrapnel through my body. "Brisa's venom is trying to get you to do what it wants, which is *not* what you want."

Because it's not what I want . . . right?

The reasonable part of me knows that these horrible pains won't last forever, but that part seems to be growing smaller by the second. I open my eyes to blinding light. Since the sun has officially set behind the mountains, the light should be dimming, not brightening. It must be another ridiculous side effect of the venom and only strengthens my pounding headache. The agony grows until I throw my head into the closest pillow and scream. I scream for everything I've been through, for the lies I've believed, the people I've lost, and the many mistakes I've made.

And then I scream because I don't want to be here.

This is *not* where I'm supposed to be. This isn't right. Every bit of me can't take being locked away in this tower for another second. I jump off the bed and hurl the pillow against the stone wall. It erupts in a plume of white feathers.

I have to get out of here.

My headache is only getting worse, and if I stay up here, it's going to cook my brain. This isn't a migraine. I was wrong. This is much worse. This is death. I force my eyes to stay open in the blinding light as I gaze around the room again, frantically searching for something I could use, but it's too sparse. I kneel at the bed and lift at the frame, my muscles pumping with adrenaline and something else––something not human. I'll throw the furniture through the door if I have to. Whatever it takes to break free of this misery, I'm game. I don't care who I hurt or what I break as long as I can get out of here.

I can picture it now. I'm breaking down the door and careening down the spiral staircase until I can find a way out. Or I'm smashing through the window and diving into the lake below. It would take a long jump to reach it, and there could be rocks down there that would kill me on impact, but I'm willing to take that risk. Death would be better than this torture, and if I don't die, then I'll be free and can find a graveyard. This is an old village surrounded by similar ancient cities, so there's got to be loads of graveyards nearby. As soon as I step foot in one, I'll dig if I have to, or I'll find a crypt.

Are there crypts that go underground or catacombs in Italy like there are in France? I hope so, that would make it so much easier, but either way, I'm not staying here.

My hands shake, and sweat beads on every inch of my skin. "How is it getting hotter?" I scream as I heave at the heavy bed.

It won't move. I kneel down to inspect it closer and growl. The frame is bolted to the floor and, even with my superhuman strength, it's not going anywhere. I dive for the bucket instead and throw it at the glass, but it bounces off with a thud. The glass doesn't even crack, but the bucket sure does. I jump up and storm toward the windows, grabbing hold of one of the bars and wincing. They're made from silver, but they hadn't hurt me earlier. I'm not a vampire yet, so why are they hurting me now? I shouldn't be allergic. I try again, but it's the same outcome. The metal is way too hot. It's like trying to hold onto the edge of a sizzling frying pan. I can't do it for more than a second or two.

It must mean the transition has begun.

I don't know what to do or how to get out. My panic builds, but there's nowhere for it to go, so I scream, and then I cry. And then I get back up and bang on the door.

"Hello?" I yell. "Is there someone out there?"

It's thick wood--way too thick for me to break through even with my added strength. I stop and listen intently, my hearing kicking up a notch. Someone shifts their weight on the other side.

I calm my voice to a more reasonable tone. "I really need to get out of here."

Whoever is over there clears their throat. "Sorry, but the boss says you can't come out until morning."

I grit my teeth together. According to Adrian, I need to be underground for three nights after being bit to become a vampire. Does that mean I have to be underground all three nights in a row? Last night I was passed out in a French catacomb, which was a step in the right direction. This? This is not going to help me! I only have two more nights to get this done, and the idea of morning feels a million years away. I need to take care of this now. What if I'm not underground long enough? What if I can't find a cemetery in time? What if Tate hunts me down again? No, I can't take any chances because I'm absolutely certain that this venom is either going to transform me or it's going to kill me.

And I don't care about the naive do-gooder girl I used to be––she seems like a shadow of a person, a girl who didn't know anything about the world. Who I am now would rather give in to my fate than try to fight it a moment longer. But I have to be smart because the people holding me captive will never see things my way.

"That's not what Tate told me," I lie, keeping my voice steadier this time. "He told me that we'd be going to dinner and to get changed." I force a smile and hope the man on the other side of the door can hear it in my voice. "Well, I'm all ready now and getting hungry."

"Don't listen to her," another voice says——a voice I know like the back of my hand. "She's a liar."

"Felix," I cry with relief, "you're here. I'm so glad you're here. You've got to help me." He doesn't respond, and I continue, hoping he can recognize the desperation in my voice and will want to free me from it. "There's been a big mistake. It's not what you think."

He scoffs bitterly, and I can picture his face full of shame and anger. "Am I going to have to listen to you all night? Because guess what, babe, there are five of us out here and more throughout the castle and outside. Everyone is on duty tonight. You're not getting out of that room."

I deflate, and then rage takes over. Did he just call me babe like it's an insult? "You have no right to lock me up! If you ever cared about me, you wouldn't allow this bull-shit to carry on."

"I *cared* for you. Past-tense." My heart twists at his cruel words. "But it turns out, I didn't actually know the girl I cared for, so shut up because you'll get no more sympathy from me."

I growl and bang on the door again, but it's useless. I can't get out. I'm locked away like Rapunzel in her tower. But Rapunzel was a princess who needed a prince to save her. Not me. I'm a powerful woman destined to become an even more powerful vampire, and no man is going to stop me from my destiny. My headache starts to ease, and it gives me a chance to think this through. I sit down on the bed and close my eyes, my mind whirling with everything that's happened and everything that needs to happen. I've got to come up with a plan. There's got to be something I can do.

And then it hits me. I haven't been patient enough. Tonight's a lost cause, but I'll get another chance tomorrow. In the meantime, I think I'll punish Felix.

CHAPTER 5

I spent all day in the catacombs searching for Eva, but she's gone. So I return to Versailles again, hell-bent on finding Brisa's blasted laptop. When I couldn't find it last night, I'd left in frustration, but now I can't figure out my next steps without it. My plan had been to find Eva and get back to New Orleans. Things were going to be a mess for a while, and getting control over my city was my priority.

But now that I can't find Eva, I need the information from Brisa's servers. She's the only one who had the kind of access I need to figure out where Eva could've gone. I know for a fact she'd tapped into the CCTV cameras all over the world, Paris included.

I storm into the palace, no longer caring what I may face, stopping by the throne room first because that's where things really got out of hand yesterday. I wonder if any of them are still in there, still fighting for something that means little without a royal blood bond. The one person I don't expect to find?

Mangus.

I stop in my tracks, staring at the very brother who was announced dead by my queen only two nights earlier. He's lounging on Brisa's old throne, long coppery hair a mess, his Victorian clothing wrinkled, and blood glistening on his lips. He blinks up at me through hazy red-rimmed eyes.

"I know," he says, raising his glass of blood-wine. "Don't tell me. You thought I was dead."

If I didn't know better, I'd think he was half drunk, but alcohol doesn't do much to our systems, not unless consumed profusely. It could be that my brother has been on a binge since his wife was murdered.

"So Brisa lied?" It doesn't make sense. Why would she lie about him dying? Did she want to punish him somehow? Sebastian was ordered not to lie, so he must've truly believed Katerina killed her husband. It's a puzzle with pieces that don't fit.

He nods, long and slow and tortured. "In a way, she lied. Truth is, brother, she really thought I was dead."

"How?"

He cuts me off. "And then she killed Katerina." His voice is hoarse. Murderous. "I'm glad the queen bitch is dead. Good riddance."

He spits and then sinks further into the throne. I eye

it warily, a pit forming in my stomach. He must see my trepidation because what he says next surprises me. "Come to take it?" His tone is lazy. He stands and sways to one side. "It's yours."

"I don't want it. I know better than to put that target on my back. You should too."

"What's the point?" He scoffs. "Let them kill me."

"You don't mean that."

He shrugs. "Maybe I do."

He's really broken up about his mate, but I understand and I can't say I blame him. So many times I have wanted to end this endless existence, but I was forbidden from ever doing so. Now that my maker is gone, I could. I won't, there's too much to do, but Mangus can, and he very well might.

"Nobody has been crowned," he goes on, "and from the ashy scene I stumbled into yesterday, nobody will be."

He's right, of course. Even if someone were to try and make a go of ruling our court, they'd be doing it through force and not a royal blood bond. Everything has been splintered, and taking that role would be like signing up for an early death. Even for a prince such as myself. *Especially for a prince.*

"Four of the lower vampires went at it right after she died and ended up killing each other." I'd stayed back, letting them pick one another off while I looked for information. Mangus hadn't even been there. But he's here now, and it's a marvel he's still alive in his state. Anyone with a grudge against him could easily take him out. The man is barely standing.

"Where's Sebastian?" I ask. "Did he die too? Do you know?"

"No clue. Maybe. Who cares? Technically you and I are the highest-ranked left," he says. "I half expect you to kill me." He raises his hands wide and smiles. "So please, do me the honor."

"I won't be killing you, Mangus," I say. "And if Seb is alive, then he's ranked just as high as we are."

Mangus frowns. "True. Ugh, our other siblings were always so awful, weren't they? I truly hope Seb is gone too. He was no better than Hugo, and Hugo was the worst." He cackles, and then his energy shifts from drunk and disorderly, to full of rage. He's not as affected by the alcohol as he wants me to believe. "But I didn't kill our brothers, and neither did my wife. We were framed. You know that, right? It was a setup. Had to be."

"I believe you." Against the odds.

I've never seen him so upset, never seen him cry. Until now. "Who would do that to us?" Tears cut down his cheeks, mixing with his stringy unwashed hair.

I'm momentarily stunned, and then I speak. "Someone interested in toppling the vampire court. Look at us now, brother. We're prime for a take-down. But that's not why I'm here." Mangus and I aren't close, but we haven't had any quarrels either. He worked with

Brisa in a traveling capacity and may be just the person to ask for help. I hate asking for help, but I'll do it for Eva. Anything for Eva. Underneath his grief, there's a powerful and vengeful creature——one I can use to my advantage. "Come," I nod toward the exit. "Let's discuss our next move in private."

Most of the court has fled, but a few wayward vamps still stick around, waiting for someone to tell them what to do. Many have lost their masters, and therefore their way. But that will change once they get a taste of freedom.

Mangus leads me from the throne room to his private quarters, throwing open the door and plopping down on the rumpled bed. The man is normally so well put together, so stoic, so hard. This is not the Mangus I know. But I understand——when Kelli was murdered, I had been lost for a few weeks. I'd lose my mind if something happened to Eva. And my dead wife has haunted me for centuries. But we also don't have time for him to unravel completely, not if we're going to secure a future for our cause.

I close the door behind me. "We need to control this." I don't lead with my goal of finding Eva. There's another angle I go for instead.

He stares at me with unblinking eyes. "I thought you said you didn't want the throne."

"I don't. It won't work anyway. Anyone who dares to take it will end up staked."

"Exactly why I was sitting on it." He says it like it's a joke, but there's truth in his words.

"You really want to die?" I point outside. "Then step into the sun."

"Maybe I will, brother."

It's a common command from masters to their prodigies to forbid them from attempting anything suicidal, and the depression of immortality fades after enough time. I didn't think it would, thought that the adage "time heals all wounds" was bullshit, but I had been wrong. Still, I don't know what to say to Mangus right now, so I say nothing. We stay in silence for a good five minutes before he speaks.

"Okay, I'll help you," he relents. "But I can't make any promises."

"That's fair."

"So what's your big idea, Adrianos?" Only those who've known me the longest call me by my full name. It reminds me of when I first met him in the 10th century. He'd been so different back then. So *angry*-- Katerina had softened him.

"We need to establish a council of coven leaders."

He sits up with a rueful smile. "Brisa forbade us to even speak of this."

"So you're glad she's gone, too?" It's a gamble to talk about her this way to another one of her children, a gamble that pays off.

He jumps up from the bed. "Of course I hated her,

but didn't know you did as well, you were always such a kiss-ass."

"We all were, Mangus. But yes, I hated Brisa for centuries." I level him with a stare. "What she did to your vampire wife? She did the same to my human one." This is hard to talk about, but I press on. "And orchestrated it to be by my own hands."

I'm grateful he doesn't ask for clarification, but his face falls, and rage flashes through his eyes. If anyone gets it, he does––I hate that he does, but I can't do this alone. "Okay, I will help you so I can have a measure of revenge on Brisa's legacy before I join Katerina in death."

My spirits fall. I don't want this for him, and Katerina wouldn't either, but I know better than to argue with Mangus. He's even more stubborn than I am.

"We need to break into Brisa's files." I give him a knowing look because while it's a secret the man has made a point to adapt with technology, it's not a secret he's been able to keep from me. If we can't find her computer, then surely she has a cloud of information somewhere. And if anyone can hack into that, it would be the man who's taken it upon himself to learn everything possible about technology. "We won't be able to form a council if we don't have the names of every coven leader."

Part of his job was to travel around and enforce Brisa's laws, so he's got more connections than I do, but even he doesn't know everybody.

He strolls to the armoire, throwing it open and retrieving a black laptop. "How could this have gotten here?" he teases.

I laugh. It's like every holiday has been wrapped into one. "You're the one who stole the laptop?" I rush toward him with an outstretched hand, but he holds it away from my grasp.

"First thing I did when I felt her die." His eyes glitter with rage and despair and the littlest bit of triumph. "I busted into her office and snatched it. Had to kill a few of her guards to do it. You're not the only one who knows that what Brisa has access to will be useful."

I step back, leveling him with a hard gaze. "We need to call a gathering of the coven leaders. Virtual or in person, I don't care, but it must be done."

His eyes narrow. "What's all this about, really?"

"The safety of our covens and preservation of everything we've worked for," I'm quick to respond.

That's only part of my reasoning. Finding Eva is dependent on getting Brisa's CCTV access. I'd tried to find her scent but couldn't, so it's this or let her go, *and I can't let her go.*

But besides that, I really do want to establish a council rather than grapple for a hollow throne. Vampires need to hold onto our prosperity in order to keep our people well-fed without the unnecessary bloodshed of humans. That's the only way we're going to stay alive--because if we start a war with them, they'll rise up against us. So many of my kind have forgotten just how many humans there are.

But as much as I should be worrying about that right now, I can't keep my thoughts away from Eva's well-being. She's out there somewhere, scared and full of Brisa's venom. If I don't get to her, something terrible could happen. God willing, I'll be able to track her down and get her to safety. She has no idea what she's dealing with, and if I don't find her soon, then I've already lost.

"How's our girl doing?" Tate's voice wakes me from a fitful slumber, and I sit up in a sweaty pile of torn blankets and white feathers. The morning sun filters through the windows in streams of golden light, and I have to blink a few times for my eyes to adjust.

"Last night was horrible." My voice cracks. Tate nods in understanding and hands me a tall glass of ice water. The condensation alone makes me want to weep.

"Drink this. It'll help." He sits down on the edge of the bed, and I gulp the water down like I've been days without a drop. "What happened last night? Is there anything you need to tell me?"

"You already know . . ." my voice trails off as I catch sight of Felix in the doorway.

He won't meet my eyes, and I can't say I blame him. Bits and pieces of last night rush back to me, and I grimace. I said so many things to him that I wish I could take back. I told him about Adrian, about the things we had done together and how it felt to be with him, and I spoke as if becoming a vampire was so much better than any human life I could have. I stand to shake out my limbs, but I don't go to him because I know I don't deserve his forgiveness or sympathy right now.

"I'm so sorry, Felix." That's all I can say, but it won't be enough. It wouldn't be if I were in his shoes.

He doesn't reply, and his gaze still doesn't reach my eyes. A hollow sadness seeps through me because I know this is the biggest turning point in our relationship so far. We'll never be lovers, and we'll likely never be friends again either.

"The venom will do horrible things to people," Tate cuts in. "It'll make you say and do things that you wouldn't otherwise."

I nod. "It was like being burned alive. I would've done anything to make it stop, but that's no excuse for the things I said."

"The desire to turn is not going to go away until you make it past night three. But the good news is, you only have to get through one more night of this."

"And then what? I really won't turn into one of them?" Because what if on night four it starts all over again? I don't think I can take a lifetime of trying to fight this off. I'm one person during the day and someone else entirely at night––and that nighttime Eva will eventually succeed in her efforts.

"No, you really won't turn into one of them unless one were to get its hands on you and start the process all over again."

A huge weight lifts from my shoulders. "I'll do everything in my power to stop this from happening again, but you have to understand that I never wanted Brisa to try and turn me in the first place." My voice catches. "They lied to me. I should've known they were going to lie to me." The room goes quiet for a minute, and I remember what he had originally asked. He wanted to know if there was anything I needed to tell him, and there is. I hate that there is––I want to scrub everything about last night from my mind, but I have to face this. "The thing is, Tate, last night I made a plan to run away today, but now that the sun is back up, running away is the last thing I want to do. In fact, I'd rather you keep me locked up until we're sure this is behind us."

Felix's brows furrow, and a flash of annoyance mars his face. He thinks I'm lying, or that I'm sucking up to Tate, but I'm not doing either. This is the real me, not that monster from last night who said horrible things to him. I'm not that girl who planned it all out, imagined every scenario of getting out of here. Those scenarios frighten me now because I'd been one hundred percent serious about getting to a cemetery and killing anyone who got in my way. I would've killed Felix, no questions asked, and he knows it.

"Can I go to the bathroom?" I nod toward the broken

bucket on the floor. "And maybe I can get a few things to eat?"

"Of course," Tate says, "we'll make sure you get three square meals while you're with us." He points to my tattered dress. It's been through so much over the last two days. "And I'll get you some clean clothing. I'm sorry that we didn't have time to take care of that yesterday. I should've had them leave you pajamas in here for when we arrived, but it slipped my mind."

That doesn't matter to me so much as food does. My stomach rumbles, and I sigh because I know what I have to say next. "But besides those few things, I think it's going to be better if I stay locked in here most of the day, just in case."

Tate nods approvingly. "I'd hoped you would say so. We don't have a lot of experience with this kind of thing. Believe it or not, most people who get turned don't leave their graves unless it's because we find and stake them."

A shiver runs through me as I imagine what a stake through my heart would feel like. I sigh, grateful to be alive. "Well, I'm glad I made the cut." And I can't help but wonder why . . .

"It was like I turned into a different person." I shiver inwardly, remembering how quickly my personality had changed. "Last night was . . ." I trail off because I don't have words for my behavior and I'm ashamed of how it all went down, even though I know it wasn't entirely my fault. The venom was stronger than I ever could have anticipated. No wonder new vampires are bloodthirsty little demons. If that's what it feels like to be turning into one, then actually being one would be ten times worse.

"Where's your thanks, huh? If you were anyone else, we would have killed you by now," Felix chimes in, his eyes finally meeting mine, and I shrink back.

"I hate vampires, and I always have. You know that about me, Felix," I challenge him with a hard stare.

"Do I?" His glare is pure fire as memories flash between us.

"Nothing I've been through has changed that," I say. "In fact, it's made me hate them even more."

"Keep telling yourself that," he replies bitterly before storming away.

My mouth pops open as I watch him walk away from me, and Tate squeezes my hand. "Give him some time. He'll forgive you."

I snatch my hand away and shake my head because I know that's never going to happen. Felix hates me now. In trying to save him and my other friends, I ended up betraying his trust. Worst of all? I betrayed myself as well. I may have learned my lesson the hard way, but at least I learned it. I'll never trust a bloodsucker again, especially not one with golden blond curls and bottomless blue eyes.

· · ·

The day goes by excruciatingly slow, anxiety gaining traction with every passing hour. Last night was the most painful night of my life, and my gut tells me tonight's going to be worse. The phrase "it gets worse before it gets better" is the one thing I'm clinging to because once I'm through with all this I'll be a more powerful vampire hunter. I'll be able to better defend myself, and hopefully nothing like this will ever happen again.

I can feel it's true––my vision is crystal clear, my senses are unimaginably heightened, my muscles are relaxed but strong, and my mind is razor-sharp. Maybe this is why Tate is taking such great lengths to keep me human. If he succeeds, I'll be a powerful weapon against the vampires. I hate the idea that he's using me, but right now, he's the only protection I've got. If I run away from here now, I'll be a vampire by morning. There's zero doubt about that.

By early afternoon, the lack of quality sleep catches up with me. I ease into a long nap, but it's ruined by the venom because when I dream, it's of Brisa. In the dream, she's a mother figure to me and I love her deeply, and when I wake up, I hate her even more. Even if she's dead, her venom lives in me, and I'll never be free of her.

Hugo's bite had made me stronger, but Brisa's venom is on another level. She not only bit me, but she exchanged our blood as well. As the queen, Brisa was the most powerful vampire in the world, surely staying human with her venom in my blood will have unintended consequences. I just wish I knew for certain if she is dead or alive. I think I burned her up when my hands glowed, and if I didn't, she's going to hunt me down and kill me.

A hulking guard opens the door and offers me a steaming bowl of pasta with tomato sauce. "Are you hungry for dinner?" he asks in a thick Italian accent.

My stomach growls in response, and he hands me the warm bowl.

"The chef is a local woman who uses a family recipe, so you know everything is fresh and authentic." He smiles, and I almost can't believe it. Shouldn't he hate me too?

"Thank you." I return his smile and twist the fork into the noodles, lifting a bite to my mouth. The rich flavors caress my tongue, and I devour the food. "Please give her my compliments."

The guard beams and waits by the door for me to finish up, then takes the bowl and leaves me locked up again. Despite the panic building, my stomach is finally relaxed. A few minutes later, the guard returns to offer me some water and to escort me to the bathroom one last time. I take it all in stride, returning to my Rapunzel tower for my final night.

Tate greets me at the door. "We're going to have more guards here tonight. We've had time to bring in as many reinforcements as we could spare. You have nothing to worry about. We've got your back."

"And who is 'we'?"

"We are a family that is highly invested in you, and that's all I can tell you for now."

I roll my eyes but don't try to fight him because I need the investment. Who else is going to lock me up in a castle so I don't end up killing myself? But I'm no fool, I know there's going to be a price to pay later. He's going to want something from me when this is over. But right now, it's one step at a time: focus and survive the night.

I thank him and head into the room. "You can lock me away now."

"Is there anything else we should do to protect you?" His bushy eyebrows rise considerably. "Anything else you can think of that we may have missed?"

I gaze around the room. Everything is sparse and neatly in order, but that only reminds me of the mess I made last night. Someone came in and cleaned it up while I was eating breakfast this morning, but I don't want them to have to do that again. "Actually, I think you should leave me the mattress with the top sheet and that's all."

He chuckles like I just made a joke, but I don't find anything about this even remotely funny. I bite my tongue from lashing out while I pull up the blankets and begin throwing them into the hallway. Felix is standing there when I do, the pile of fluff landing at his feet. I haven't seen him since this morning, and my heart lurches. He's so handsome, so familiar, and so very hurt by me.

"You're back," I say tentatively.

"Not for your sake," his response is cold. "It's my job."

"Really? Because I think you should be in New Orleans attending university."

"I don't expect you to understand loyalty to a cause," he quips. "My education can wait, this cannot."

Sure, school can wait, but that doesn't mean it should. Felix deserves better than to be standing guard over me. "Shouldn't you be loyal to your lacrosse teammates? To your studies? And your future?"

"Everything I'm doing is for my future." He turns away and folds his arms over his broad chest, effectively ending the conversation. There's nothing I can say to get through to him, and my skin is starting to buzz like it did yesterday on the drive into this place, so I leave him to pout and go back into the tower room.

"Good luck," Tate says, locking me in once again. A sense of foreboding crawls up my spine and sinks into my chest, pounding on my heart. This night is not going to be easy, and there's nothing I can do about it. I just have to force myself through it, because the alternative is out of the question.

CHAPTER 7

The sunset feels like a doomsday countdown, and I wonder if I'm about to say goodbye to the sun forever. Could this be my last sunset? Am I really going to make it to the other side of this night with my humanity intact?

I know what's about to happen, but that doesn't make it easier when it hits me. A headache slams into me like a freight train, quickly transforming into a migraine and then into something much worse. It's so excruciating that I have no words to describe it. Maybe I should've kept the blankets because the room is brightening, and even though I'm squeezing my eyes shut, light is still assaulting me. Tears spill from my eyes, and I pray for numbness to take me.

That doesn't happen.

It's as if my soul is clinging to me for dear life and I

don't know how to save it. Either I die a human or I lose my soul because this pain can't be tolerable. It just can't be. My body is impossibly hot, and I scream out in frustration. I'm frantic, and that feeling just keeps getting worse with each quick breath of my lungs. I can't handle this. I can't, I can't, I can't. I thought I could be strong enough to do it again, but I'm not. And it's not what I want.

I want to be a vampire.

The thought hits me with stark clarity, easing the pain enough for me to focus on it. I want immortality. I want power. I want what they have, whatever is on the other side of being a human who can hurt and feel too much. It's going to be so much better than *this*––I'll do anything to get it. Whatever I'd said to Tate was foolish and naive. I was a stupid girl who feared the very best thing that had ever happened to her. Queen Brisa gave me a gift. A queen wanted me as an heir, and who am I to squander the chance?

I sprint to the door and begin begging for someone to let me go. "Please," I gasp, "I've changed my mind. I promise I won't hurt anyone, but I need to get out of here. I'm going to die if I stay up here." My voice rises. "I'll die. Do you want me to die? Are you murderers now? You can't just keep me against my will!"

Nothing.

I don't expect Felix to understand, but whoever else is on the other side of this door doesn't say anything either. I should've asked the guard who brought me food to give me his name. He seemed kind, like maybe he would help someone in need. And he's huge, probably big enough to take on the other men if needed. "Please," I go on, "I swear, I need to go to the hospital. I'm not going to make it." I know they're there. They have to be. But they ignore me, and I hate them for it. Maybe I will kill them when I get out of here. I'm going to make them regret leaving me in this kind of pain. Anyone who can sit there and keep me trapped in hell doesn't deserve to live.

I scream in agony and then go quiet, scurrying to sit next to the door and wait for an opportunity. If I don't make a sound, they might check on me. I need to be in a prime position in case that happens. But waiting is excruciating. My blood burns through my veins, quickening with each breath. My gums hurt so bad that I can picture two little fangs trying to break through them, and I wish they would already.

If I could rip off the door right now, I'd set them on Felix for locking me in here. He should know better than anyone else. He's supposed to be my friend, and here he is, putting me through something as terrible as this. I picture myself ripping into his lovely flesh and striking a thick pulsing vein. His blood would pour into my mouth like liquid salvation, offering me a new life. It would taste divine, and I wouldn't stop until I'd sucked up every last drop. He'd have to die, of course, but that's all part of the life cycle. Everyone dies. It's sad but inevitable, and what are humans for if not meant to feed vampires? And Felix smells so, so good.

I'm lucky to have been bitten by Brisa. I'm going to get out of here and become a vampire without anyone to tell me what to do. Brisa will be my master, but she's not here, and she might be dead. And if that's the case, then I'll be free to feed as I please and do whatever I want. I don't have any blood bonds to anyone else who could tell me what to do or force their ridiculous vampire rules on me. Felix will be my first kill, but he won't be my last.

There's a commotion outside the door, and my hackles rise. Someone yells, footsteps pound, and shots are fired. I jump to my feet and ready myself.

"They went that way." I hear Felix say as his voice fades beneath the sound of his retreating footsteps.

I stay impossibly still as the blood rushes through my veins. A long minute later, the handle wiggles, and then the door creaks open. I blink in surprise at the vampire standing in the doorway. I immediately recognize her as one of Brisa's many minions, but I don't know her name. She's tall and slender, with warm brown skin and thick ebony braids. She's dressed in all black and sporting a wicked grin. Whoever she is, I instantly love her.

"There you are," she says coolly. "You need to come with me."

I'm quick to follow her out. "Does this mean Brisa's alive?" I ask with trepidation as we hurry down the stairs. The woman doesn't answer me as she practically floats down them, but I don't have that ability yet, and my humanness makes me slower than she is. I can't wait for that to be gone. Part of me is hopeful my maker will be able to greet me upon my transformation, but the other part wants to live my vampire life as I wish, including feasting on as many humans as I can. I know Brisa's way of things, and I don't like the thought of them.

When we make it to the basement garage, the vault door is wide open, and a cool breeze greets us. I sigh in relief. We step through the door, and I grow giddy with excitement. The garage door has been blown clear off its frame, and the promise of night and graveyards and warm sweet blood calls me forward.

The woman points. "East of the city is a graveyard, but they'll find you there come morning."

"Won't I already be a vampire by then?"

She shakes her head. "You might, but we can't risk it. We need to go further in case you need more time underground to make up for what you've lost." She lifts me easily into her arms even though we're probably the same weight. Of course, that means nothing to a vampire, I'm light as a feather to her. "There are several places I can take you."

"Does this mean Brisa is alive?" I repeat my question as she takes off. To human ears, my voice would be lost on the wind, but with her excellent hearing, that doesn't matter.

"No," the woman replies sharply, and my mouth falls open. I knew it was a possibility that I had accidentally killed her, but to have it confirmed leaves me feeling mixed up. It's like I'm waiting for a favorite meal and watching it cook behind glass oven doors. I can smell it, imagine it, wait for it––but I won't be satisfied until I get to taste it on my tongue.

The woman continues to run with me in her arms. She's impossibly fast, and the landscape blurs around us. With a jump, we're over the castle wall like it's nothing. And then we're running along a path on the cliff's edge. The lights of the village twinkle, and a soft smile plays at my lips as I watch them fly past. Soon this will all be a memory.

Something as dark as the sky appears in our path and knocks us to the ground. I cry out in surprise as pain shoots up my arm when I land on it. On one side of us is a farm field, on the other is the cliff with the lake below, and standing over us is a man. I adjust to his presence and growl under my breath.

"You!" the woman screeches. "Where have you been? Sebastian's been looking for you."

"I don't answer to Sebastian," he replies in a gruff tone. "But I can see he sent you to do his dirty work. Where is my brother? I thought he might have died with the others."

My heart tugs at the sound of that all-too familiar voice, and I scramble to my feet. Anger is quick to grab hold. "Adrian," I sneer, "what are you doing here?"

Because it's him––and I am so damn angry at him. Despite wanting to be a vampire now, I'll never forget what he did. Maybe I should be thanking him for giving me over to Brisa like a piece of meat, but thanking Adrian has never been my forte.

He turns to me and smiles softly, his light eyes practically glowing. "Nice to see you too, Angel," he says, "but unfortunately, not under these circumstances." He's so fast that his movements blur. He knocks the woman out with a single blow to the side of the head, her body crumpling to the ground, and then he pushes her over the cliff. Her body hits the lake with a splash. I jump up just as he turns on me with a fierceness I've come to recognize.

"What are you doing?" I growl.

"She was going to make sure you turned," he snaps. "Or she would've killed you. One or the other."

"Did you just kill her? You can't kill her. She's helping me."

"She'll be fine. Now tell me, how exactly was she helping you?"

I hold up my hands. "You wouldn't understand." All he knows is the girl who hated vampirism, he doesn't know the real me.

"I think I understand perfectly," he frowns, a look of regret passing over his sharp features. "I feared this would happen."

"I want to be a vampire," I challenge, "I know better now."

He shakes his head once and pins me with a cold glare. "That's not happening."

I have two choices. I can stay and fight him, or I can run. I choose the latter, taking off in the opposite direction.

The cold soil and pointy sticks of the empty farm field fly out around my bare feet. I'm in nothing but thin cotton pajamas, but that doesn't matter. I am free, *finally free*, and Adrian is threatening to take that away. I'm fast--the speed at which my muscles are pumping me forward is far beyond anything I've experienced before. I was a track star in high school, but this is a zillion times better. It's a taste of what my life will be like soon, and I'm reveling in it. The world around me fades to the background as I run at such a high speed that it's almost as if I've already made the transformation.

This is it. I'm going to outrun my captors, outrun the man who betrayed me, and find a graveyard all on my own. I have the whole night to do it. Since it's November, the sunset was early, and there are hours of night left. I smirk and urge my body to move even faster, Brisa's venom fueling me. It doesn't matter that I've hated vampires all my life, that everything about me will change, and that I will lose the friends and family I have left. This is right where I'm supposed to be--and I get to spend an eternity with total control.

Too bad Adrian is faster.

He jumps on my back and we tumble to the ground. "You need to stop this nonsense, Angel. This isn't what you want," he commands as he lands on top of me. His flesh is a welcomed cold, but only because I can't wait to join him in immortal life--not that I will have anything to do with him in my next life. I want nothing to do with Adrian now, and I'll want nothing to do with him later.

"You have no more say over anything I do ever again," I snap, shoving him off me. I jump up to run again, but he isn't having it. He growls like a damn wolf and pulls me into the cage of his arms. His body is solid steel--despite my own amazing strength, it's not enough to match his. He holds me tightly against him and levitates us into the air.

"No," I scream, kicking out and trying to wiggle free. "Unless you're taking me to a graveyard, you need to let me go."

"No can do."

My mouth goes dry. "What are you doing?"

"I've never seen anyone take to the venom quite like you have," he grumbles, almost talking to himself. "If I'd known you were going to be so adamant about turning, I would've . . ." He doesn't finish his thought.

"You would've what?" I snap, angry at his antics. He's acting as if he isn't the reason I'm here in the first place. "Nothing. You wouldn't have changed a thing."

"That's not true."

I don't believe him, but I don't say anything more, and neither does he as he flies us back toward Tate's castle. As we get closer, though, I give into my fear and start to beg. "Please, Adrian. Please, if you ever cared for me, even a little, please don't take me back there."

"This isn't you talking."

"It is," I squirm. "It's me. You know those people can't be trusted."

For a moment, his arms loosen and I think he's going to let me go, but instead, he leans in close and whispers hotly against my ear. "As much as I hate Leslie Tate, that man has the safest place for you to make it through tonight."

"You can't be serious." My heart thuds wildly in my chest at the mere thought of being locked up in that Rapunzel tower. It will ruin everything.

"Do you think I want this?" His voice sounds pained, but I don't feel sorry for him. He's the one taking my choices away, not the other way around.

"I don't know what you want," I seethe, my hatred of him growing tenfold. "And that's all that should matter. What I'm telling you right now should matter."

My mind races back through my time with Adrian.

I'm disgusted by the vulnerability I showed him. He didn't feed on my blood, but he fed on my emotions, and it was only a couple of nights ago that he happily took my virginity, all while spinning lies to deliver me to his queen. Brisa didn't want her newest vampire princess to be a virgin, and Adrian had seen to it that she'd gotten exactly as she'd asked for. I know now that she'd planned to kill her princes off--and had already gotten started--but Adrian didn't know that when he'd taken her orders. He probably still doesn't know seeing as she had whispered that confession to me.

"I hate you!" I scream. "You've done awful things to me just because you wanted to do them. You're vile!"

"I'm saving you now, aren't I?"

"You should listen to what I want. This isn't saving me. This is ruining me."

He tightens his grip, not responding to that. But it's true, it's all true. He's done what *he* wanted all along. Sure, the royal blood bond made it so he had to do what Brisa asked, but he's worked out ways to lie to her before, and he certainly seemed willing to take me to bed. The very least he could've done was find some way to warn me about what was going to happen, or at least act upset when she revealed her plans. The man didn't even apologize. "The truth is, you don't love me and you don't even care for me. You made me into a fool!"

A fool who fancied herself in love.

A fool who gave her body and heart over to her enemy. A fool who cherished that night as if it had actually meant something real. Turns out I was wrong, but I will never make that mistake again.

Anger rolls through me like a tidal wave. He doesn't get to win again. As we near the castle, I thrash out, trying to gain purchase--one last ditch effort to get away. But it doesn't work because he's simply too strong. Adrian has already broken my heart once, and now he's doing it again. It never seems to matter what I want, everything he has done in our relationship has always led to him getting what he wants and me getting screwed over.

"If you're smart, you won't let Tate know that I'm alive," he whispers against my ear. "They still don't know what vampires survived your attack, and it's better that it stays that way."

My attack? I was laying there on my deathbed with light blasting from my hands, and he's calling it an attack. "You've got to be kidding. I'm definitely going to tell him you were here," I reply, sounding childish but far past the point of caring.

"Do that, and you'll be facing the consequences more than I will." He doesn't even have the decency to sound bothered.

I'm not sure what he means, but the truth is, I probably won't be telling Tate squat about anything. I don't trust him either. He's only helping me because he wants something from me. Fact is, nobody has my back in this world. Nobody. Not even Ayla, because she broke off our friendship. And not even that vampire woman who's currently passed out in the lake, because no doubt she only helped me to suit her own plans.

I hope she comes back for me.

Adrian clamps his hand over my mouth as we slow to a stop. We're still flying––at least fifteen feet up. His scent normally makes me want him, but right now it makes me hate him. I look down to find we're hovering over a group of Tate's guards. They are standing just outside the castle, talking about where I could've gone. If only they'd look up, they wouldn't sound so worried by my disappearance.

Why do they care if I become a vampire, anyway? I'm not going to bother them. Sure, I have no plans to be chummy with vampire hunters, but I plan to keep to myself. Maybe I can get enough control over my thirst that I'll eventually only feed on the bad humans. I can hunt them down and make them pay for the awful things they do. But I won't be feeding on blood bags. The idea of it seems so lackluster, like having a rubbery fast-food hamburger instead of a prime filet mignon.

A thought strikes me––if Brisa is really dead, does that mean vampires are free to feed as they want? The bloodlines won't be erased entirely because they'll fall to whoever is highest in the pecking order. Adrian doesn't have any vampires below him because he hates taking on prodigies, but other vamps have suckers under their control. Will they enforce blood bags and stick to Brisa's laws? Or will they give in to their base instincts? The human part of me fears what this could mean, but that's nothing compared to the thirsty part of me, and that part agrees with the old way of doing things.

"Don't say I never did you any favors, Angel," Adrian whispers, his lips soft against my cheek, and then the bastard drops me.

The inertia of falling shoots a tremor of fear through me. I cry out before I can tap into my common sense and keep my mouth shut. I hit the earth hard, landing on my butt and getting the wind knocked clear out of my lungs. It isn't more than two seconds before Tate's guards are on me. There are at least ten of them, and they surround me on all sides, pinning me to the ground like I'm a common criminal.

"Where the hell did she come from?" someone asks. I recognize Seth's voice straight away. He sounds like his usual angry self. I'm surprised he's here, but I guess I shouldn't be.

"She fell out of the sky," another adds with a laugh. "Lucky us."

"Doesn't matter, she's here, isn't she? Carry her back upstairs and lock her up again," Felix's voice rings out, and my stomach turns to rocks. There isn't an ounce of sympathy in his tone.

"No!" I scream, "You can't--"

Seth clamps a large hand over my mouth and glares down at me. I glare right back, thinking that he never did like me. He's probably loving this. I thrash my limbs about, trying to get away, but I can't fight these men off. It's no use. There are too many of them and only one of me. My only hope is that another vampire will break me out before sunrise, but with Adrian hanging around to see to it that I stay put, my chances are eroding to dust.

They carry me upstairs and throw me back into my tower. As Felix slams the door in my face, terror rips through my body. I run to the window and scream obscenities into the darkness.

CHAPTER 9

ADRIAN

I hover outside of her room, my black cloak camouflaging me into the blustery night. Her light is off, but that doesn't matter, I can see everything as if it were the middle of the day. To say she isn't doing well is an understatement. She's livid and attempting to break free, but it's not going to work. I'm keeping watch over her and won't let her transition to my kind even if she hates me for it. And maybe she will hate me, maybe she already does, maybe she always will, but I can't go back on my promise.

And yet . . .

The second I wrapped Eva in my arms tonight, I knew my suspicions were correct––saying no to this woman is next to impossible. It's never been easy, but something about tonight felt vastly different. It felt like she had finally taken control of our relationship, and in a way that left me defenseless.

Could it be because we've slept together? Reminders of what it feels like to have her, even though I don't deserve her, keep returning to my mind and warming my body. Or maybe it's because she's becoming more powerful than me. I can't stop thinking about that either. Either way, this woman has a way of getting me to do what she wants. And this need to go to her and free her from that tower? It's killing me, but I refuse to give in. I live on my own terms and always find a way to make my life what I want of it, and that includes keeping my promise to the bad-mouthed woman who stomped into my office months ago, hating vampires more than anyone.

No, I'm sticking to what I know is best, so I won't go to her. My hands ball into fists and my chest aches with frustration, but I stay where I am, determined to see this through. I will not allow her to sway me in this. I will not let her change my mind. Nobody will have control over me ever again. Not even Eva.

I spent centuries building up a tolerance to Brisa's bond and now that she's dead, my problems are even bigger, and Eva is the center of them all. Asserting my free will is more than important to me––it's everything. Losing that was what I'd hated most about having to answer to a master, and yet here I am completely undone by a nineteen-year-old *human*. Alright, turns out she's not entirely human. Her blood is mixed, but it's still close enough.

And nineteen? *Nineteen!* What is wrong with me? I

can't have someone my own age because nobody my age exists, but I make a habit of dating women older than nineteen. Doesn't matter that my body is permanently frozen at twenty-four, everything else about me has grown the kind of bitterness that can only come with age. Eva isn't a child, but she's vulnerable and soft under that hard exterior. She deserves better than me.

But damn it if she doesn't bring something to life that I've not felt since I was a mortal man. I don't often think about my human life. The memories are tainted, and it's so far in the past that sometimes I forget what it had even been like to have those mortal needs. But when I do remember, I'm reminded of everything I've lost. Some in my coven like to call me a sadist, but even I can't wallow in that kind of misery for long. Those horrors aren't something I seek out because when I think of my lovely wife Eleni and our unborn child in her womb, the images of their bloody deaths claw at me, taking me to my darkest places.

They'd died at *my* hands.

I'd murdered them. My bloodlust had been too much. Brisa had turned me and set me loose on them without me having any clue what was happening, and then she tricked me into believing she could help me feel better. I've lost so much because of that monster, but she's gone, and I am still reveling in her death. I wish I could have seen the moment it happened. Her loss is both devastating and exhilarating. My vampire nature makes it impossible not to grieve, but I'm free of her too, and she'll get no tears from me.

Nor from the sick bastards out there who will use the opportunity to undo everything Brisa has built--that I helped her build. We've only been public for eighteen years, but preparing took decades longer. And now what? How many vampires feast on human flesh? Will they kill their donors or let them live? Will they turn whoever they please, sending us back to the Stone Age? Mangus was able to get his hands on the genealogy, and a meeting has been called for one week from today. I'm worried things won't go the way I need them to, but I have to try.

Mangus was also able to get me access to the CCTV, but I'd had to tell him who I was looking for. He didn't bat an eyelash. I was surprised--I'd had the impression that he didn't care for Eva. But he said he understood and left it at that, and then I'd come here on my own. I'm not even sure where Mangus is now. The man doesn't have his own coven to keep his death wish at bay.

I shake my head, once again angry at Brisa for all she's done to those I care about. It's the emotion I can't seem to be rid of. Here I'd spent the weeks in her palace trying to convince her to hold off on making Eva one of us, and she did it anyway. Clearly, Brisa hadn't worried about the risks enough to see reason. I'd suspected what Eva was, and Brisa had confirmed it the moment they met. So why didn't she leave well enough alone? Eva isn't meant to be one of us, and in trying to turn her, she could become our biggest threat.

I watch her now, pacing in her little tower like a mouse in a cage, and plan ways to kill her or turn her. I won't, but I should, and so I plan. Does she realize how much trouble she's in? And how much trouble she could cause? My vampiric nature urges me forward, and I move closer to her window. I'm strong enough to get in there. I could do it before talking myself out of it. It would simplify everything. With her gone, I could return to New Orleans and take control of the city. Who knows what will happen with the rest of the world, but my coven is my coven, and they'd stand with me. As the most powerful vampire in New Orleans, the other vampires will be given a choice: swear their allegiance to me or get out.

Some will leave. Most will stay.

Eva stands at the window, eyes searching the darkness. When they land on me, she stops and sneers. "Let me out of here!"

She can see me. The guards will assume she's talking to them, but I know it's me she hates right now. And she shouldn't be able to see me in the dark like that until she's turned, but then again she has a lot of venom in her system. The desire to kill her morphs into the urgency to turn her––make her one of us, so I can have her forever. She could come work by my side, making her hometown into whatever we desired. We'd have so much control, nobody would dare cross us. Time is so fleeting, moves so quickly, and I could––

"––Please," her voice softens, a whisper meant for my vampiric ears only. We stare at each other across the space, and I want to go to her, the need is so heady, my fingers itch.

"No," I whisper back, and then I levitate up above her tower, looking down so that I can see and hear everything below but she can't see me.

She spews obscenities that sound nothing like her, and I force myself to calm down. I need to be stronger. Better. I'd almost gone through with turning her twice tonight. The second I'd picked her up and flown away with her, those thoughts had raced through my mind. I'd fantasized about burying her in a cemetery and being there when she rose as one of us, welcoming her into my arms. Right after I'd pictured giving in to my basest desires to sink my teeth into her soft flesh. Now that Brisa's commands are null and void, it's something I could do, something maybe I should do . . .

Stop it. I shake my head, trembling with my lack of self-control.

I will do none of those things because Eva has gotten under my skin and into my cold dead heart, and it's become my job to keep her safe. It no longer matters if she hates me, that's unavoidable, and I'm used to being hated anyway. I am a man of my word if nothing else, and I'd promised her she won't be turned. I intend to keep that promise.

She continues to yell, but I close my eyes, drowning her out. I can't listen to this, it's too tempting. Too heartbreaking.

My thoughts return to two nights ago. It had nearly killed me to leave Eva there with Brisa and the others, but I couldn't watch my failure happen either. Brisa hadn't commanded me to stay, so I'd slipped out like a coward. Since that moment, it's been days of self-loathing. Days of plotting.

"So help me, Adrian!" Eva's voice startles me. "I need you."

I don't respond. She has no idea who's after her or of the trouble she's caused, because if Sebastian is after Eva, that means the others haven't forgotten about her either. They'll be wanting revenge on the beautiful creature who murdered their queen. Or they'll be wanting to use her for themselves.

"This isn't my fault. Why should I have to suffer?"

She's right, it isn't her fault, but by tomorrow night she'll be in the clear. I'm going to get her out of here and away from Tate. This little tourist trap certainly isn't the fortress I expected of his kind. It'll be simple. But for now, Tate has the best place to keep her under lock and key while this third night passes and her humanity is preserved. She needs to be locked above ground, and as much as I hate to admit it, I can't get close to her right now. My urges are too strong. To feed. To kill. To turn. To do anything but let her become my greatest enemy.

It's better than being one of us. This fate is evil, and

I've hated giving it to others. Kelli was the last. And now that Brisa can't control me, I'll never turn another human again. Certainly not Eva. Never.

I observe Tate's guards assembling below the castle. The man himself must be close by, maybe even under this roof, though I can't be sure. This could be my chance to kill him once and for all, but that would require I leave my watch over Eva. I can't do that. Nobody else can keep her as safe as I can. Nobody else can see as much as I see, or hear, or smell, or sense . . .

At least I know what Tate's people are up to. I know his family and what they're capable of. No doubt they will use Eva against the vampires––and so many others. I can't have that. My coven needs me, and I need her, alive and mortal and by my side. Tomorrow night. One more day. I can be patient. I'll kidnap her if I have to, take her kicking and screaming, but she's leaving Italy.

Evangeline Blackwood is mine.

CHAPTER 10

I stay awake until dawn, as salty beads of sweat drip down my face. I feel as if I'm trapped in the Sahara instead of sitting in Northern Italy on a blustery November evening. My body is stiff with panic and slumped with exhaustion. Bloodthirsty thoughts swirl in my mind, and it isn't until the night disappears that I relax.

The sky fades from black, to navy, and then lights up with hues of pinks and golds like a promise at a new life. One thing is for sure--I'll never ever let something like this happen to me again. I don't care what it takes. I go to the window, testing the silver bars against my fingertips. They don't burn. I lean against them with a long sigh. I can't see the sun from my tower, but I can feel it wash through my body like a healing balm. Tears blur my vision.

I survived. I can't believe I survived.

Relieved, I stumble back to the bare bed and drift away into sleep. I'm too tired to think about everything that happened last night for another second. I know Felix and Seth will never forgive me, Adrian saved me from myself, and Tate is only helping me for some long term gain--but none of them matter more than my desperation for sleep right now.

When it greets me, I don't dream of Brisa. Instead, I dream of Adrian, of his hands on my skin, his lips on my mouth, and the heated way his gaze lingers on me. I've never seen him look at anyone else the way he looks at me. It's like I'm a puzzle he can't quite figure out, but he wants to. He's not bored or annoyed. He's intrigued. He's amused. Does he love me too? My heart believes I'm in love, but that emotion quickly shifts to anger when I wake up. Our relationship was built on lies, and seeing him last night brought that to the surface. The truth still remains--Adrianos Teresi is no good for me.

"Knock, knock." Tate pokes his head in the door. He's all fresh in business casual clothing, and his pepper hair is slicked back. He looks like he had a much better night than I did. "Are you okay?"

I groan and sit up, rubbing the remaining sleep from my eyes. "Nope, but I'm still human, so at least there's that."

He enters the room, followed by more guards than he had yesterday. They crowd in around me, eight in all. The fit men and women are dressed in black with guns and stakes strapped to their bodies. I guess Tate was serious when he said he was calling in reinforcements.

"You did it." He smiles broadly. "Congratulations."

I nod once, but at my primal center, I know that I'm not meant to be locked away. It's not who I am. But I also know I'm not meant to be some disgusting bloodsucker. "Thank you for helping me survive the venom."

"It's my pleasure, Eva. And now that I know you're safe to be around, we're leaving here. This location has obviously been compromised." He pauses. "Do you know what happened to you? Who helped you and why did you fall out of the sky like that?"

"Vampires." I shrug. "One helped me leave and one intercepted me and brought me back."

His eyes flash with surprise and he rubs his chin. "Do you know who they were?"

"No. I didn't get a good look and they didn't speak." My cheeks heat with the lie.

He considers this for a long moment and I'm not even sure why I'm keeping Adrian's name out of my mouth, except that I don't trust Tate.

"Very well," he says at last.

"So where are we going next?" I don't expect him to be forthcoming, but I can't help but ask the question. The guards back up to give me space, and my cheeks warm when I realize they're all staring at me like I'm a ticking time bomb. Felix and Seth are among them, and they're the only ones who aren't staring at me like they're afraid of what I'll do next. In fact, they don't look at me at all.

"We could keep moving you every day or two and try to stay ahead of the vampires," he says, "we have enough real estate."

"That sounds kind of fun, assuming I could see Italy along the way." I smile ruefully. I already know it's wishful thinking, but I'm trying to be positive here. And I really am grateful I'm still me. I wouldn't have made it through this without Tate. Whatever he is, at least he's good enough to have helped me survive.

"But . . . I think it's best if we take you to one safe stronghold and hide you there."

"I had a feeling you were going to say something like that."

"Yes, well, it's for the best. The family helicopter has been made available and will be here within the hour. We'll be at our new location within three."

Family helicopter? I swallow hard, trying to imagine what kind of family has a helicopter. But then again, Tate had enough funds to set up an elaborate hunting organization in New Orleans, so he must have deep pockets.

"Okay," I agree to the plan, the idea of playing tourist deflating like a birthday balloon.

Tate must see it on my face. "The vampires will still want you. They could try to turn you again, though, I don't expect it to work." He frowns at the thought. "You may not know this, but there's only so much your body can take, and you've already lost a lot of blood. If they tried again anytime soon, you could end up dead."

My stomach hardens.

"But my guess is they won't attempt to make you a vampire again."

I know exactly what he's getting at. "If they can't have me, then they'll want me dead?"

He nods, and we don't say another word about it.

According to the vampires, I'm too powerful to be anything but one of them--well, except for Adrian. He obviously doesn't want me to become like him. And maybe I should tell Tate about Adrian showing up last night, but I decide to keep my mouth shut. I still don't know Tate's angle.

"Let's get moving," Tate announces, heading for the door in two purposeful strides. I follow him out and spend the next hour showering, changing into comfortable clothing, and eating breakfast. When we head out to greet the shiny black helicopter, I think what a shame it is that I never got to tour the castle, swim in the lovely lake, or explore the quaint village. I hope that's not fore-shadowing what the rest of my life will be like--watching the world from behind the safety of Tate's protection.

The chopper lands in an open field, and four of us climb inside. My heart lodges in my throat as we rise quickly into the cloudy sky. We zoom over the rocky countryside, and I hang on tight to my seatbelt, simulta-neously uneasy and exhilarated. I've never had an experience like this, and it's too bad it's under such crappy circumstances.

A few hours later, we descend toward our destination. I didn't recognize much of northern Italy––it was stunning, and I'd love to return someday––but this landscape? This, I *do* recognize. For some reason, I'd expected to go to Rome, visions of the Colosseum dancing through my head, but we're quickly approaching the colorful Amalfi Coast. Even in the off-season, this view is right out of a storybook. A smile bubbles up as I take it all in. I've seen the famous coastline from viewing travelers' viral posts on social media, but to witness it in person is an entirely different experience. It steals the breath from my lungs.

The imposing mountains are dotted with granite rock faces, with white and tan buildings nestled between. Some of the rooftops are yellow, orange, and blue, but most are muted natural colors that blend into the rocky cliffs. The Tyrrhenian Sea sweeps over the horizon like a blue blanket, even more pristine than the lakes up north. The air is slightly warmer here too. Italy must be wonderful during the summer months, and I envision the beaches full of happy tanned people who get to lay out under the sun before venturing into the historic city to enjoy the rice Italian culture.

Too bad I need to stay hidden from the vampires. As much as I'd love to explore this coastline, I'm sure Tate won't allow it. And anyway, I can't stay for long. I need to find a way back home. I need to call my mom and make sure she's okay. I need to check in on Ayla because even if our friendship is on the fritz, I still care for her and want to repair things between us. I have a life to get back to, no matter all the crazy things that have happened to me.

We've got headphones on to protect our hearing, but they're not offering much support, and I foresee a headache on my horizon. I look to Tate where he's lazily reading an Italian newspaper. Pressing a button on the side of the headphones, I'm able to speak to him. "I need a phone," I say, "I need to call my mom. She's got to be sick with worry."

He drops the paper and gives me a nod. "One step at a time."

"You can't keep me from my friends and family."

"And I won't." Then he's back to ignoring me, this time reading something on his cell phone, seemingly unaffected by the picturesque landscape zipping past us and by my demands. Except for the pilot, there are only two hulking guards sitting with us. I know they're here to keep us safe, but they still make me a little uncomfortable.

Tate said the other guards will be driving over to our new location, which means Felix and Seth will be showing up again soon. I appreciate that they came to save me from Versailles, but I don't want them here on my account. I don't want to mess up their lives anymore.

Tate gazes up from his phone and nods to a building

that stands apart from the rest. My jaw drops. "Is that where we're staying?"

"Now that we're sure you're not a vampire, you can join us in our family home," he responds. "This place is special."

"I'll say." It's not a quaint castle with a tower up top that could double for a princess's hideout, and it certainly doesn't look like a home either. It's a fortress––big enough to be a grand hotel and surrounded on all sides by a massive stone fence with silver pickets all across the top. There are guard towers at each corner of the fence, and when I squint I can make out the people there standing watch. The footprint of the structure itself takes up most of the space, but I catch sight of a few courtyards and a green lawn off the back. The building's walls are a sleek whitewashed limestone with rows of silver-barred arched windows. This place screams "old money" and "no vampires allowed" at the same time.

I turn on Tate. "You aren't mafia, are you?" I immediately regret asking so openly. People who value their lives don't just go around asking their captors if they're in the mafia. Even though Tate's helping me, he's still my captor. I couldn't get away if I tried. Unease gnaws at my chest. This isn't good.

He raises his bushy eyebrow and smirks. "We don't need to resort to criminal enterprises to keep our lights on."

I swallow hard, remembering how my mother got

involved with the mob back in New Orleans. The memory of getting my head slammed into a wall echoes at the back of my skull, a reminder of what it felt like to lose control over my life. I'm lucky to be alive after everything I've been through. More than lucky.

"I know you're wondering who 'we' are," he says ruefully, "and I've said that we couldn't tell you until it was safe." I sit up straighter, ready to hear more. "Answers will only have to wait a little longer." He holds up his hand to stop me from interrupting. "Be patient, Eva. I promise it's all going to come together soon."

CHAPTER 11

"Eva, welcome to Casa Del Sole!" A young woman with a slight French accent bounds from the house, and I immediately recognize Remi, one of my servants from back at Versailles. I blink at Remi in surprise, stopping in my tracks. She laughs and tugs me in for a quick hug. "In case you hadn't figured it out, I was a spy," she stands back and winks at me. "And I'm so glad you got out of there. I was getting worried about you."

Her curly blonde locks gleam in the sunlight, and behind her is the endless blue sky. Like Tate, she doesn't have an aura. I already knew that about her, but the confirmation that she isn't human puts me on edge. I inch back, unsure if I can trust her. Being a spy just means she's good at lying. And she's Tate's spy, not mine.

Tate was willing to sacrifice my friends. He'd sent all

of those hunters into the casino for a chance to get at Adrian knowing full well people were going to get killed. It's only because of my deal with Adrian that they weren't slaughtered. Whatever he and Remi are, they're not human. They risk lives, they haven't been honest with me . . . and I'm probably one of them.

Whatever that means, I still don't know. If I ever want to find out, I need to play their game, so I plaster on a fake smile. "Oh, right, Remi, it's good to see a familiar face." My voice comes out weirdly chipper, and I have to stop myself from cringing.

"Come on," she says, "I'll show you to your room."

She takes my hand and tugs me after her, guards following at our heels. Tate's phone rings, and he stays back, nodding at me to go with Remi.

"You're here early enough in the day that I can show you around first," she says.

"Sounds good."

Casa Del Sole is even larger than it appeared from above. It really could be a hotel, except I'm sure it's not. Tate called it the family home, and with the guard towers and loads of silver accents, I'll bet whoever lives here is mortal enemies with the vamps. Silver is hard to come by, it's expensive, and the suckers have a vested interest in getting rid of it, but these people have an abundance. We walk into a grand entrance through silver doors twice as tall as I am. I don't know what I expect, but it's not what I find . . .

People.

There are people walking through the corridors––at least twenty. They look at me and smile, and some even wave hello.

"Is this place open to the public, too?" I ask, confused that Tate thinks this is their most secure location. The touristy castle ruse obviously didn't work, so to try another tourist destination seems like a bad idea.

She shakes her head, her hazel eyes widening. "Not a chance. Tate really didn't tell you anything, did he? Casa Del Sole is . . ." She ponders on her words for a second. "Well, think of it like someone's home where they've also set up an exclusive boarding school."

Okay, what? "This day is full of surprises."

She laughs. "Come on, let me show you around."

"How old are you?" I ask as she leads me into a library with golden light streaming through the windows. "You look too old to be in boarding school."

"I'm twenty-two. I finished my time here already and stayed on to work for the family."

"Oh yeah, tell me about this family."

Her smile beams. "You'll meet them soon, I'm sure. Don't worry, you're going to love them. They're an old Italian family, and they find people like us and help us."

"People like us?" My fingers itch, so I ball them into tight fists.

She winks but doesn't say more on the matter. I drop the subject for now and let Remi show me from room to room. There are two classrooms, a grand dining room with a long table that seats at least fifty people, a state of the art gym, a light-filled center courtyard that doubles as a greenhouse and is brimming with exotic plants, and even an elegant indoor pool.

"There's an outdoor pool too," Remi says dreamily as we stand at the edge of the chlorine-blue water. "We spend loads of time there in the summer, but it's already closed for the season."

"Just my luck." Summers in Italy would be my fantasy. It's hard to believe people live it in real, everyday life. "How many people live here?"

"Well, the family comes and goes, but this is their main residence. There are eleven of them in total, including the matriarch who is the actual owner of Casa Del Sole. Her husband passed away, but she has three grown children, two of which are married, and five grandchildren."

"Tate's one of these people?"

"He's the son-in-law. His wife has a couple of brothers."

"And then they invite people like us to stay here and study with them?"

"Yup. Right now, there are seven students under their tutelage. And then there are tons of security guards who live here full time, plus the household staff, two teachers, some admin people for the school like myself . . ."

"So you're an admin who moonlights as a spy?" I raise an eyebrow, and she goes pink.

"Come on. I'll take you to your room." Her abrupt

change in subject is so jarring that I don't say anything more as she grabs my hand, but I quickly shake her off. I'm sure my hands are sweating.

"Are you okay?" she questions. She stares at me, and I realize my mind has softened against my will with that one touch of her hand. I so want to tell her I'm not okay, to unload all my worries on her, but I don't let myself give in. If she's trying to do something similar to what Tate can do, I don't want any part. But I also don't want her to be suspicious that I know what she's up to, so I nod and lie through my teeth.

"Yeah, this pool just looks amazing. I was thinking of how nice it would be to jump in right now. I don't normally like swimming, but this summer was so busy that I missed out on the fun." I'm totally rambling.

"There will be plenty of time for swimming," she laughs. "Come on now, let's go to your room."

I stare longingly at the cobalt blue pool as she drags me away. A strange feeling comes rushing right back with her touch, but I don't shake her off again. I'm still not sure how I feel about her or this place. On one hand, Casa Del Sole is beautiful and welcoming, the kind of home that existed only in my dreams. But on the other hand, I'm not sure how safe I am here. And I want to go home. I miss my mom, and I really miss Ayla.

A thought strikes me as we pass by a pair of what I think are students. They're close in age to me and say hello as we pass, then scurry off around one of the many corners. "You know I'm not enrolling here, right? I'm only staying for a little bit to get away from the vampires until things die down. I'm going home soon."

Remi gives me a pitying look. I know what she's thinking, that I don't have a home to go back to anymore, that nowhere is safe for me now that vampires are after me. But she doesn't understand how badly I want to return to normal. Why should I be punished for something Brisa did? I was forced to leave New Orleans––but what about my new apartment? What about my mom? My life? I've got to find a way to get it back.

"Think of this place as a vocational training program instead of a school. People come here at all sorts of ages, but most are college-aged young adults like us, which makes it more fun. You might actually be interested in what we do here after you learn more about it." Her voice drops. "And about yourself." Her eyes are practically bugging out of her head, and I know she wants to tell me more.

My mouth turns to sawdust as I consider her words. If I'm like them, that means this is a place for energy demons like Tate. Are they here to learn how to drain humans? I'm not about to trade becoming a blood-sucking vampire for an energy one. So far, I haven't seen a single aura, so I can safely assume these people aren't regular humans, not even the guards or the staff. And just because I may fit in here, doesn't mean I want to.

"Does this have something to do with the fact that none of y'all have auras?" I blurt out, then my mouth pops open, and I drop her hand. "Maybe I shouldn't have asked that. I'm not good at knowing when to shut my mouth."

She grabs my hand *again* and tugs me into my room, closing the door. The room is on the top floor and bigger than any bedroom I've had before, with pretty wood furniture and white linens. A large window overlooks the coastline, and same as at the castle, there are silver bars fastened across it. But I barely have time to take any of that in, I'm more concerned with whatever Remi's doing to me. Her touch makes me want to talk, to trust her with all the fears I normally keep to myself.

"How much do you know?" she demands in a whisper. "Tate said you don't know anything, but you obviously do."

My hackles rise, but I can't help from spilling my guts, hoping this burden won't be mine to carry alone anymore. "I know that Tate sucks energy from humans and that he's not the only one. I've seen people like you without auras doing it before." My voice goes impossibly low, and my heart pounds. "I also know he can make people do things or forget things. It's a lot like vampire compulsion."

Her lips thin, and guilt shadows her pretty face. "Okay, so you know a lot. Full disclosure, I'm supposed to report anything you say back to him," she says, holding up her hands and finally dropping mine.

"So don't," I reply. This time, I fold my arms and tuck my hands against my sides.

"I have to do my job," she says sheepishly.

"So can Tate do that manipulation thing on you too?" I tilt my head at her. "Is that why you have to do your job? Or is it that you want to do your job?"

"Both," she shrugs, and that's all I need to know.

No more telling my feelings to someone who's going to go blabber them all to Tate. At least now I know not to trust her with any secrets. "Fine, but at least tell me what he is, and what I'm guessing you are too? Because in my head, I've been calling you people energy demons."

She gasps and murmurs to herself in French. "We are not demons!"

I shrug. "Then what are you?"

A knock sounds on the door, and we both jump. Leslie Tate strides into the room. "How are you settling in, Eva? Feeling okay?"

"I'll leave you two alone to talk," Remi squeaks out, and then scurries out the door. I can't come to grips between the woman who was my maidservant back in Versailles and this jumpy girl. How could she have been so brave in the face of vampires but acts so skittish around Tate? Is she afraid of him? Intimidated? He must have more power over her than he does over me, which I'm pretty sure has something to do with the venom.

I turn on Tate and rest my hands on my hips. "To answer your question, I'm fine, but I'm ready for you to tell me what's really going on."

"Remi explained what we do here?" he asks, circling

the room. Is he going to ignore the fact that Remi practically ran out of here?

"In a way." I raise a brow. "She showed me around and said it's like a vocational training program." I level him with a hard stare. "But she wouldn't say what for."

He stares right back, as if weighing all possibilities in his mind. I'm waiting for him to do his manipulation trick on me to test if it will work again. I don't think it will work as well as he would want it to.

"You're to stay away from the students and out of the classrooms for the time being," he says abruptly. "You're here because we need to keep you out of the vampire's hands, and that's all for now."

I scoff. "Why can't you just tell me? I already told Remi that I know about you sucking energy from humans, I've seen it. And I know that you can compel people similar to the way vampires do."

"That's a special talent of mine personally," he answers. There's frustration lacing his tone. This man isn't used to being talked back to. "So you can see why the family has decided to make sure you can be trusted before letting you in on the secrets."

I balk at him. "See! This is what I mean. Do you know what I am? Am I different from other humans?"

He heaves a heavy sigh. "It's not all up to me to give you these answers. But again, once we're sure you can be trusted, you'll be the first to know. In the meantime, you'll be safe here."

"Really? Because it feels like I'm here to be your prisoner. The same thing happened with the vampires."

His eyes flash. "And does any part of you miss the vampires? Do you feel yourself being drawn to them in any way?"

Memories of Adrian come to mind, and I squash them.

"No, of course not, but I feel like we're in a game of chicken right now. I can't trust you until you tell me the truth––so how am I supposed to act like I can be trusted? You already know I hate the vampires, but you act like I don't."

He laughs at that.

"What's so funny?"

"You left New Orleans with a vampire prince! And then you played dress-up with the queen and her court. And now you have the oldest and most powerful vampire venom in your veins. So forgive me for being skeptical."

"You picked me up, not the other way around." I glare, a fury building inside me, but I have to admit his reasoning makes sense. That still doesn't make up for the fact that I did those things because I was forced to. "None of that was my choice."

My face heats remembering my time in bed with Adrian, something that was most definitely my choice. A bad one, but still mine. Everything else, though? Not my doing! A little voice in the back of my head is yelling at me to cut the shit and take accountability for my part, but I silence her.

"Be that as it may, my family has an obligation to protect our interests."

Here he goes again with the "family" talk. I step back and release the wind from my sails. This conversation is going in circles. If I act appreciative, then maybe Tate will loosen the reins a bit and I can figure out what an energy demon actually is. Remi acted like calling her a demon was a slap in the face, so they must be something else.

"You win," I say, defeated, "tell me what to do, and I'll do it."

Words I never thought would come out of my mouth. But the more I'm around him, the more I'm reminded that he's in the power position. He brought me to this fortress, and I'm not sure if the monsters outside of its walls are any worse than the monsters inside them. I have to play nice and get his family to trust me, which means I'll have to hang on to his every word and act as if he walks on water. The man has an ego the size of Texas, and I should've realized this about him the day we met.

He smiles like he's just won our little game, but I'm not done playing. "Today, you will lay low and keep to your room." He heads for the door.

"And tomorrow?" I ask, hopeful.

He stops and turns back to me. "Tomorrow, you will meet the family."

CHAPTER 12

*A*fter a long nap, I wake up renewed and ready to take fate into my own hands. There's a walk-in closet and a chest of drawers filled with clothes in my size and, figuring they must be for me, I rummage around until I find a black one-piece bathing suit and matching cover-up. I change and set out for the indoor pool. I'm not really interested in swimming as much as I am looking for a good excuse to explore this place on my own.

When I leave my room, however, I'm met with the same two guards who accompanied Tate and me in the helicopter this morning. Neither of them have auras, both are middle-aged and rippled with muscles, and they've practically got "no-nonsense" written on their foreheads.

"Where are you going?" the first guy asks in a thick

Russian accent. The second one just grunts and looks me up and down like I'm a security threat.

I motion to my outfit. "Swimming."

"Did Tate approve this?"

I roll my eyes and play it cool. "I need some exercise, and Tate only said the classrooms and other students were off-limits, so the swimming pool should be fair game." I turn on my heels and head in that direction, half expecting them to drag me back into my new room, but they follow behind and don't say another word.

So much for exploring, they're not going to let me out of their sight. I guess I shouldn't have expected anything different, but I'm still disappointed. I remember where the pool is, but I take a wrong turn on purpose to see what the guards will say. They're quick to correct my error.

"I thought you said you wanted to go swimming?" the Russian asks gruffly.

My cheeks redden as I turn around. "I do."

"This way then." He nods toward the opposite corridor, and I follow after him. I've got myself sandwiched between these guards, and I'm itching to get away from them. They're here to watch me more than to protect me, and I'm not used to being around anyone this much. I've been a lone wolf type of girl for years. I was good with Ayla when I needed a friend, but enjoyed being by myself a lot. Being followed like this isn't something I'm too keen on.

When we get to the pool room, it's blissfully empty. I

release a sigh, thankful that I don't have to deal with even more people. The large room is lined with gleaming white tiles and the pool is long, thin, and bright turquoise. It's only a lap pool, but that's fine by me. It's also deep, and the reflection of the water bounces off the low ceiling. If I watch it for too long I'll get dizzy.

I remove my cover-up and dive in. The cold water washes over me, and I'm instantly able to let my worries go. I'm not big on the cold, so normally I would screech like a drowned rat in this temperature, but something about today feels infinitely different. Maybe it's the venom or the change in scenery, or simply doing something as normal as swimming, but I love this cold pool.

I swim laps for a while, getting lost in my thoughts before allowing them to wash away with the water. My body is fluid as I pump from side to side of the pool, and my muscles warm up. I've never gone this fast. I feel like an Olympic swimmer and imagine myself in a race. Maybe I should've joined the swim team in high school instead of running track because this is amazing. I could be off winning championships with some university scholarship right now.

I know it's the venom, but it's still fun to imagine.

"Hey, watch out!" A voice breaks me from my daydream, and I stop, my head bobbing on the surface.

"Do you mind?" another voice adds. Staring down from the side of the pool is a group of two guys and two girls about my age. One of the girls points to the pool water. It's swishing so hard that big waves have lapped up onto the pool deck. "You're going to get the towels wet."

I blink in surprise. I hadn't realized I'd been swimming so fast and had displaced so much water. It must be the venom that's made me stronger than I'm used to. "Oh, sorry." I sink back down into the water. I don't know why I'm embarrassed––I usually don't care what people think––but I am, and it's annoying. They strip down to their swimsuits and jump in, and I wade to the ladder to climb out.

"You're the new girl, right? Evangeline? We've heard about you." One of the guys catches me before I go. "I'm Gentry." He has an American accent, and something about that makes me feel like I'm not so out of my element here.

"Gentry, don't talk to her," the girl from before chastises him. "My family hasn't approved of her yet. You know the rules."

So she's one of them . . .

I'm not surprised that they've been instructed not to talk to me, and it's not like I need to talk to them either. They may look like normal humans, but I know better. None of them have auras! I can't let myself get manipulated again, and who knows what kind of powers they have. Tate can manipulate minds, and Remi was trying to do something to my emotions. The girl got me to admit my energy demon theory. My hackles rise as I realize I'm not safe around these people.

Gentry shrugs and grins at me, dimples popping in both of his cheeks. He's a home-grown American boy type, and nothing I can't deal with if we're just talking about appearances. But who knows what kind of powers he could have. I suck it up and return his smile, shaking his hand and testing to see what happens when I touch him.

Nothing. *Thank goodness.*

"Hi, Gentry. Yep that's me, but call me Eva. Only my mother calls me Evangeline."

"It's nice to meet you."

"That's enough," one of my guards cuts him off and points to me. "Time to go."

"That's what I was doing." I roll my eyes and climb from the pool, shooting Gentry a genuine smile. "It's nice to meet you too."

Is it nice to meet him, though? I don't think anyone here can be trusted. It's not lost on me that seeing human auras was an ability that came with venom, but I'm glad I have the ability now. It's one of the vampire defenses to be able to tell humans apart from whatever these enemies of theirs are, and now I can tell the difference too. But if these people are the suckers' enemies, does that make them my allies?

Ugh . . . I don't even know anymore, and I certainly don't want to face the reality that I could be one of them, even though it's time I face it. It's not as if I want to sign up for this school, but it would be nice to have some answers for once.

I dry myself off with one of the fluffy white towels and leave these kids to it. I hurry back to my bedroom and shower just in time for a late lunch to be delivered to my door. Four mini triangle sandwiches are piled next to a handful of berries and grapes, and my stomach grumbles just looking at it.

The guard hands me a couple of water bottles. "Do you need anything else for the night?"

"Oh, so I guess this is dinner too." I sigh and set the food and water down on my bedside table. I know Tate wanted me to lay low, but I didn't expect to be so shut off from everyone. "How about a phone?"

"No can do." He shakes his head. "Anything else?"

"You people are really starting to piss me off." I widen my eyes. "I need to call my mother, and nobody has a right to keep her from me, not even Tate."

"Sorry, kid. This place is a sanctuary for a reason. None of the students have phones."

"I'm not a student."

"Nope."

I throw my hands up. "Alright, what about television? Or books? Something to keep me from dying of boredom?"

He strides past me and opens the nightstand drawer, retrieving a thin remote. With the push of a button, a gold-framed print of the Italian countryside flickers on. I had no idea it was a television; who has a television that looks like artwork? This place is next level.

He hands the remote over. "We're not trying to make

your life harder," he says, "in fact, we're doing the opposite. Think of how hard your life would be if you weren't somewhere safe the next time you want to complain." With that, he leaves, locking the door behind him.

I roll my eyes, hating that he's right, and get to eating while flipping through the channels. Most of them are in Italian, so they're no use. Why is it that most Americans only know English, myself included? Other countries teach people multiple languages in school, but ours doesn't. I find that quite annoying at the moment. Sure, I picked up on a little Spanish from the Moreno family, which sounds similar to Italian, but I still have no idea what the people on the TV are talking about. I study the remote harder and locate a button for a streaming service.

Thank heavens it works. I settle into a new series, hoping it's binge-worthy enough to get my mind off everything. Luckily the show is funny, and the best part? It has absolutely nothing to do with supernaturals. I think I've had enough of them for today.

$\mathcal{D}$arkness comes, and I go to bed relieved that I'm not trying to make myself into a vampire tonight. I sleep better than I have in weeks, but I wake up the next morning feeling like a different girl--one who is angry at herself for being so selfish.

Here I've been, worried about the venom in my veins, when innocent people are in trouble. It's time to stop resenting the venom and see it as the asset it is. Humans are my priority, and that isn't going to change. In fact, I'm more determined to end the vampires now that I know how cruel they can be. And heartless. They'll always see humans as food to be played with and then consumed. It's not going to change, and neither will I.

I can run and hide, spend the rest of my days trying to keep away from them now that I'm a weapon against them, or I can turn that weapon on them just as they fear. I'll do more than just defend myself. I'll become the best vampire hunter the world has ever seen. I'll hunt them down, one by one if I have to, until they're wiped from the earth. And what's more?

I'll get the word out about the venom. There have got to be more people like me out there that would do anything to transform into badass vampire hunters. Why not let everyone know the big secret? It may get me killed, but it would be worth the risk. We could end vampirism once and for all. That impossible goal suddenly seems less impossible, and I grin wickedly to myself.

This is it. I can feel it.

But first, I need to know exactly what I am.

I haven't wanted to face the facts, but Tate brought me here to stay among his people because I must be one of them. And if I am some kind of energy demon soul-sucker, I need to know so I can get back to what I'm meant to be doing: hunting vampires.

I sit up in bed and eye the television. Brisa is dead, so the world must be dissolving into chaos. I turn it on and scroll until I find the BBC. I turn up the volume, listening intently to the anchors' reports on elections, natural disasters, high-profile criminals, and what seems like a typical news day. I watch for a few minutes, searching for news of Brisa's death, but there's nothing. The story must not have broken yet, but it's only a matter of time. When it does, it's going to be huge.

I watch for a few more minutes, searching for clues

until a headline catches my eye. On the bottom of the screen where the smaller stories scroll by in text is one that sends my nervous system into a panic.

Breaking: 12 dead in an apparent killing spree in Zurich, Switzerland.

That's all? There's got to be a report on this. A killing spree is a big deal, but the story slides by with little fanfare. I twist my lips and sit back on the bed. I need to look into this further because my gut says it could have something to do with vampires.

And it doesn't help that the suckers have their fingers in everything, especially the news. Could someone be holding off news of Queen Brisa's death? Then again, most people don't understand how blood bonds work, let alone the royal one.

But I know the truth.

The vampire alliances would've splintered with Brisa's death. Whole covens of vampires are probably reverting back to their old ways, and it's only a matter of time until the news of everything breaks. Maybe it will turn out to be a good thing and cause a much-needed war between humans and vampires? But with compulsion working on anyone over twenty-five, humans might not come out as the victors. In the meantime, vampires can't keep this news hidden forever. Somebody needs to warn the world. I wish that someone could be me, but I don't know how I can sound the alarm when I'm locked up here. Besides, I do need to stay away from the vampires until I'm ready to fight them.

I spend most of the day in isolation. The guards take me to the dining hall to eat meals, but only after everyone else has finished up. I don't see Remi again, and when I ask to go swimming, I'm told the pool is already in use. By the time the stylist comes to my room that afternoon and introduces herself, I'm eager for something to do. I find it strange having a stylist considering I'm perfectly capable of doing my own hair and makeup, but she insists this is the way things are done for special gatherings.

"The family has no shortage of funds and likes to enjoy the finer things in life," Kaylee says with a grin as she brushes out my hair. "Might as well enjoy it."

"The family, huh?" I look up at her from the vanity chair in my massive bathroom. "What can you tell me about this family?"

Her cheeks pale and she shakes her head. "I can't say anything, but you're lucky they're showing such an interest in you. Don't worry, you'll do great."

"You're making me nervous."

She doesn't say another word about it as she curls my hair and applies my makeup. She uses way too much bronzer for my liking, but I have to admit the woman knows what she's doing. When she's finished, I've been transformed from a nineteen-year-old who uses dry shampoo more often than she should to a sophisticated socialite. I change into an emerald green evening gown with matching strappy heels. Kaylee finishes the look off with a string of pearls.

This is so not me. And even though it's a gorgeous look, I've had enough of playing dress-up. I only want to be myself. No more pretending. Just as the sunset is painting the sky a cotton candy pink, the guards enter my room and tell me it's time to go.

"Good luck," Kaylee beams, but I can't return more than a polite thank you. My stomach tightens and my hands shake as the guards lead me downstairs and through the hallways into a much more intimate dining room than the one I've used. Unfortunately, I'm the last guest to arrive.

CHAPTER 14

Tate's the only one I recognize, but the entire family must be in attendance because I quickly count eleven people. The matriarch herself sits at the head of the table, an imposing woman with thick white hair swept on top of her head and knowing black eyes that send a shiver through me.

The grandchildren aren't young. All are probably older than I am, or close to it. I don't know why that catches me off guard, but it does. I'd assumed when Remi had said "children," that she actually meant children.

Tate stands to greet me as all eleven pairs of eyes assess me from head to toe. Some are welcoming, but most are not. They're all dressed as well as I am, and all look as if they're used to these types of gatherings. "Ah, Evangeline, please come in," Tate says, "let me introduce you to the De Luca family."

I frown at the surname before remembering that Leslie Tate is the son-in-law. I stride forward to the intimidating woman at the head of the table and extend my hand. She takes it, shaking it with a firm hold while gazing up with a sharpness in her eyes that is either judging or protective or both. It's immediately apparent that this woman is not one of those who loses her touch with age. She's quite the opposite, and can't be fooled by the trappings of youth.

"Hello, child," she says in a syrupy Italian accent. "I'm Camilla De Luca. Lovely to finally meet you."

"It's nice to meet you too," I return, and she drops my hand.

"Everyone, I'd like you to meet Evangeline Blackwood." Tate points to the people seated around the table and begins introductions. "This is my wife, Bianca, and her older brothers Fredrico and Dario."

Bianca is much younger than her husband, with a sultry untouchable energy about her. She probably married Leslie when she was fresh out of high school and had her children shortly after. Either that, or she's had a lot of plastic surgery. She gives me a tight smile—they all do. It's pretty clear that they don't trust me, but she seems particularly bothered by my presence here.

"And these are my kids, Bella and Greyson." It's strange that Tate has been living at the hunter gym without his family, but I don't comment on it.

I recognize Bella as the standoffish blonde girl from the pool who told me not to get the towels wet. Her hair is obviously dyed because her complexion is as dark as her family's. The contrasting colors suit her well. She turns up her nose and shifts away. Greyson is a bit older with long dark curls and pouty lips that turn into a full-on scowl.

"Fredrico is the oldest De Luca son, and his wife is Lainey." Tate points to the couple. Fredrico reminds me of the male version of Camilla, and Lainey is a soft plump woman who gives me a sweet hello in an American accent. She's not nearly as intimidating as the rest of them and appears the same age as her husband.

"Enzo and Nicco are their twins." Identical men in their late twenties nod to me. They're built of so much hulking muscle that they barely fit into their chairs.

"And Chloe is the baby of the family."

Chloe is the only one who offers me a genuine smile and also the only one who looks to be my age or younger. She matches her family, Italian and beautiful, with the sweet roundness of her mother. I can immediately tell she's the kind of girl who fits right in wherever she goes. When she says hello, her accent is more American than Italian, like her mother's and her uncle's.

"Thank you all for having me," I say. My voice comes out a bit shaky, and I want to pinch myself.

"Are you sure about this, mother?" Fredrico says darkly, bypassing me altogether. "She's an outsider. We can hardly trust her to join us for our family dinner."

I want to roll my eyes at that. What's so special about

a family dinner that an outsider can't be invited in for a meal?

"I trust Leslie," Camilla croons back. Fredrico's sitting right next to her, and she motions for him to move. "Go further down the table. I'd like Evangeline to sit by me tonight."

The tension in the room grows thicker, and I feel awkward as hell. This family is nothing like what I grew up with. They're the complete antithesis of my childhood. Sure, my mom and I have had a strained relationship, but we don't play games. I'm keenly aware that these people are incredibly competitive while still being close-knit.

Trying not to let my face reveal just how uncomfortable I am, I sit down in his still-warm chair. A staff member is quick to change the drinks around, pouring me a glass of wine in the process. I'm parched, but I don't touch it. If there's one useful thing I've learned from Tate, it's that alcohol is never a good idea for a vampire hunter. I go for the glass of water resting next to the wine instead. The condensation wets my hand——a wake-up call of sorts for me to not forget who I'm with. *These people could be worse than the vampires.*

"How are you enjoying your time here so far?" Camilla asks.

"I'm safe, and it's a beautiful place to hide out," I reply with the truth. "But I'd appreciate some answers to my questions. Your son hasn't exactly been forthcoming."

"Son-in-law," Camilla corrects, and Tate shifts

uncomfortably.

Further down the table, someone scoffs, but other-wise it's quiet as midnight in this room. Nobody says a word for a long minute, and then the silence is inter-rupted by staff with trays of food. They get everyone situated with heaps of roasted lamb and vegetables.

"Leslie, will you offer the prayer?"

Everyone bows their heads, and I do the same, but I'm so startled by the fact that these people are praying that I can hardly hear a word of it. Does praying make them good people? Not necessarily. Plenty of people pray one minute and then go off to do horrible things the next.

"Please enjoy," Camilla says when the prayer is over, and everyone digs in. I do as well, but I find myself picking at the food despite my gnawing hunger. Some-thing about this dinner feels like a test somehow. They're all watching me intently, as if I'm eating the wrong way. I frown at the silver forks, wondering if I should've picked up the small one instead of the big one.

"So, do you go by Evangeline or Eva?" Bella asks coyly, a gleam of mischief in her big brown eyes. "Or perhaps it's Angel?"

Hearing Andrian's nickname for me on her lips makes me pause. "Eva, thanks."

"Tell us about yourself," Enzo asks. He and his brother have piercing blue eyes that turn on me at once, and I nearly fall out of my chair, I'm so uncomfortable. It's like they can see into my head.

I clear my throat, half expecting someone to save me from talking about myself, but of course, nobody does. Talking about myself is my least favorite thing to do. I've always found people who talk about themselves instead of asking questions of others to be dull. The most interesting people are usually the quietest ones.

"There's not much to say." I shrug.

"Oh, I doubt that," Lainey replies. She's nice, but I can't help but keep my guard up. Her apparent niceness could be an act.

"Well, I was born and raised in New Orleans, Louisiana. I'm nineteen. I'm not in college right now, but I'd like to go eventually. I'm considering nursing or something that will allow me to help people. I work as a server at a popular restaurant, and I've been training with Tate to be a hunter."

None of these things are actually true anymore considering it's been over a month since I left home without a trace.

"Do you have any family?" Bianca asks innocently, and a few of the others look away.

"I'm the only child to a single mother," I say it like it's no big deal because to me it's not. "It's just the two of us."

"I can't imagine what that would be like," Chloe pipes up, her fork midair as she addresses me. "It must be so quiet."

"You're lucky to have so many family members," I say, "but then again, I'm lucky too."

"And why is that?" Dario asks. It's the first time he speaks directly to me, and there's something about the man that gives me the creeps. Maybe it's because he's a single man looking at me like I'm fresh meat, but I don't think so--it's more than that. Something I can't quite put my finger on.

"There are pros and cons to everything," I supply but don't elaborate because I don't have to defend myself.

He raises a dark eyebrow. "And what are the pros to being in such a small family?"

I level him with a stare, anger burning deep. I can't believe he has the audacity to ask me such a rude question. "When it comes to my mom, I get all the attention, all the money, and all the time. There's no one for me to compete with, now is there?"

The room goes silent, and I know I've gone too far. If they didn't already hate me, they're going to now. They have to compete for Camilla's love--of that I'm certain.

Dario glares, but Fredrico smiles, raising his glass. "Fair point."

"You're not getting attention if you're sharing it with her gambling problem," Greyson juts in, and the guy may as well have punched me in the gut. I go ghost-still, blood pooling in my cheeks. How do they know about that? I shoot Leslie Tate a scathing glare, and he frowns apologetically.

"We've done our research on you," Camilla cuts in as if her son and grandson aren't complete asses. "Don't be surprised that we had you vetted before inviting you to our table. Why do you think you weren't brought here straight away?" Her eyes narrow. "My family is under my protection, and one can never be too careful these days."

There's an undercurrent to her words I don't quite understand, a double meaning that I'm meant to uncover. All at once, she grabs my hand and squeezes. I yelp as pain shoots through me——white-hot unexpected agony that drops me to my knees beside her, my chair long forgotten. The sounds of the room fade to white noise as my head buzzes.

My life flashes before my eyes. Memories of my mother, of Gram, of Ayla and Felix, and everyone else that mattered. Early childhood and holidays and memories of school come barreling to the surface, and then I'm reliving the last three months of my life. The hell. The excitement. The mistakes. The whirlwind of falling for Adrian's tricks. The foolish agreements I made with him. The incredible joy I felt when Mom beat her addiction, thanks to him. The unruliness of Versailles. The ecstasy of sleeping with Adrian after weeks of yearning for him. The terror of being bit by Brisa. The darkness of the catacombs, and then the light bursting from my hands.

And Brisa.

Again, I see Brisa——this time, she's consumed by the light.

Camilla releases me, and I scramble back, falling to my butt. "What did you just do to me?"

"I read your memories," she answers, her gaze digging into my very soul.

My dinner threatens to come up as those four words sink in. I didn't know that ability was possible, but it's a violation I'll never be able to get past. I glare at the woman, wanting to spit in her face and run far away from this place.

Lies. It's all lies. They promise safety and then do *this*.

"I didn't give you permission," I growl.

"I don't need permission. This is my house you're in, and my protection you're under."

"But I'm your guest."

"You're here for a specific reason, Eva. Do you want safety from the vampires? Fine. I believe you. I can see how you were fooled by them. Adrianos broke your little heart."

Someone laughs, and I'm so angry, I could cry.

"You need me, and I need you." She leans down to get a better look at me. "I'll give you the safety you're craving, and the answers, the training . . . I'll give you everything you need if you choose to stay here with us."

I blink up at her in surprise. If I'm being honest, I'd never thought they'd let me walk out of here. I'd assumed that, once again, I'd been imprisoned by those in the power position. The fact that she's offering me a choice doesn't fit with her character, but it gives me an opportunity to test the waters.

"So I can leave?" I stand up, heading for the door.

"You can leave," she calls after me, "but if you do, you'll be dead by sunrise."

I stop and glare at her. "I'm stronger than you give me credit for."

"Oh, darling, I know all about your strength. Do you not think we have also taken the venom? We have. All of us."

Again––another revelation. Tonight is proving to be full of them.

"Our family has been draining fangers for generations," Dario adds with a satisfied smirk.

I throw up my hands. "Fine! If you're so great, then why don't you fight the vampires? Why train innocent humans to do your dirty work?"

"Because there are so few of us left, and we can't make more of us as quickly as they can. And, if you can't tell, I rather like my family, and I'd like to see them alive."

"So what do you want with me, then?"

"Stay here. Work for us."

I want to call her bluff, so I push my way out the door, stomping toward the exit. I need to see if she's being honest with me or if she's going to swoop in at the last moment and drop me in some prison cell somewhere. It's easy to get outside of the mansion, but not so easy to get past the wall. I ask that Russian guard who's always following me around, and he leads me right to a gate.

"Are you sure about this?" He scratches the back of his neck.

I turn on him. "If I go, are you instructed to chase me?"

He shakes his head. "You can go, but you shouldn't. Camilla will help you. She's helped all of us."

I stand there, staring out into the street beyond. Who knows what I'll find. Whatever it is, I might not survive it. I might not survive this place either.

With a groan, I march back into the dining room. I was never going to leave because I don't have a death wish, but I wanted to make sure I could. When I return to the dining room, the family is all still sitting in their chairs, enjoying their dinners as if I hadn't just left and then returned in the span of five minutes.

I point at them. "Okay, I'll stay if you answer my questions."

Camilla pats the place where I had been seated.

"Come, sit back down. Have dessert with us, and we can discuss anything you like."

I return to my chair, but I'm on high alert now. Not even the decadent cheesecake the staff brings out can distract me.

After a few bites, I set down my fork. "What are you?"

"We," she raises her eyebrows and points at me, "are not the monsters that you think we are. And you are one of us, in case you haven't figured that out, but I think by now you have."

"You steal the humans' energy and suck their lives away. I've seen it."

Her lips thin. "Then you saw wrong."

"I don't think so." I point at Tate. "I saw him in the hospital ICU. He was taking someone out with the energy-sucking thing."

"I was helping them," he counters, his voice booming across the table. He turns to his mother-in-law. "This is exactly why I wanted to tell her earlier. She's been confused. No wonder the vampires got to her."

"I had to check her memories first," Camilla challenges. "And do you know that she was spying on you for that vile Adrianos?"

His cheeks pinken, but that's the only indication that he's angry or embarrassed because his words are as smooth as satin. "I'd figured as much, but I wasn't worried about it. She didn't see anything."

"She saw you in the hospital ICU," Greyson is quick to point out, much to his father's annoyance.

Camilla releases a slow breath. "Regardless, I need a full picture before ever welcoming someone into my home. You all know that."

Tate nods once and looks away. I can tell he wants to say more. Greyson's smirk is triumphant, and it's obvious the kid resents his father. What a great family this is turning out to be . . .

Camilla levels me with soft eyes. "Eva, what you saw in the hospital was Tate helping a human. It's what we're here to do."

"I don't understand. I know what I saw."

"You saw wrong," she snaps. "Tate goes to the hospital because when someone is close to death, we can help them transition back to spirit with less pain and suffering."

"Come again?"

"We transmute painful energy, feelings of fear, grief, anger, and so on," she says. "That's what Tate was doing. He wasn't hurting that patient, he was helping them. We can't save someone from death, but we can make it easier for them to cross over."

"And that does what for you?"

"You're right that it feeds us in a way. It makes our abilities stronger."

I have to fight to roll my eyes because I also know what I saw in the nightclub and I'm sorry, but none of those humans were on death's door. They want me to believe it's all sunshine and rainbows when I know that's not true.

"Okay, so that takes me right back to my question." I raise an eyebrow. "What are you? Don't make me keep asking." And really, I'm asking what I am too. My heart beats faster, and I'm equally terrified and eager to know the answer. I really hope she doesn't say werewolf because they're supposed to have been hunted to extinction and I really don't want to be howling at the moon anytime soon.

They exchange nervous looks, and then Camilla nods.

"We are the descendants of angels," she says. "We're nephilim."

I'm waiting for someone to laugh, for a punchline to be dropped, but that doesn't happen. Looking around the room, it's clear everyone here is absolutely serious.

"Is that hard for you to believe?" Tate questions. "Many humans didn't believe in vampires when they first came out eighteen years ago, and now the whole world has accepted their existence."

"I mean--I guess--yeah, makes sense, I guess." I stumble awkwardly through my response. How the heck do I respond to something like this? And what does it mean for me?

"She's not human," Fredrico says. "She shouldn't be so surprised."

"But she was raised as one." Camilla takes my hand, and I wince, expecting to be violated again. But nothing happens. This is just one person taking the hand of another and nothing more. "You are special. Didn't you always feel that deep down you were special?"

I shake my head. The truth? I felt ordinary. Actually, I felt less than ordinary. I was nothing but a normal girl living a normal existence in a messed up world. And now I'm supposed to be some kind of angelic descendant?

It's all too much.

"Okay, so not special," Bianca says. Her eyes are cruel, and Tate gives his wife a deep frown. There's something amiss between him and his family. "But maybe you felt like you didn't belong? Like nobody ever truly understood you?"

Damn it. She's right.

Her smile lifts and she nods. "That's because you didn't belong."

Camilla tugs on my arm, and I'm forced to turn back to her. Her eyes are softer now, compassion filling them. "But we understand you, darling. We know how it feels to be different, to be underappreciated, and to have your light dimmed by the world. But you don't have to worry about that anymore because you're one of us now. Welcome to the family."

CHAPTER 16

Angels? It's not lost on me that my nickname is Angel, and now I'm supposed to believe I'm descended from one. I don't know much about angels except that they're talked about in the Bible and they work for God. That's about it. And I still don't know if I even believe in God, but I guess He or She must exist if angels do. This is all so weird...

Despite everything, I'm still waiting for them to all start laughing, to tell me that they're pulling my chain and that I'm actually something else, but they never do. They just stare at me with equal parts expectation and the kind of seriousness that means they believe they're exactly what they say they are. They want me to believe it too. And part of me does––the part that's lived among vampires and has seen things she can't explain. But the other part of me––the normal girl who didn't grow up with this stuff, she doesn't know what to think.

"Come," Camilla motions to Chloe, "show her."

Chloe stands and approaches me with glittering hopeful eyes.

"What is she going to do?" I ask.

"I'm the record keeper," is all Chloe says. She grabs hold of me and everything goes white.

Blinding white.

Then I'm thrust backward, my entire body prickling with the inertia of falling impossibly fast. All at once, it stops, and I blink as the scene around me begins to form into a desert and stone buildings and people dressed in strange clothes. Chloe is standing with me, still holding onto my arm. Her hand slides down into mine and she squeezes. "They can't see us," she says, "this is only a look into the past. None of this is here anymore. It's all dust."

"I have questions," I mutter. "So many questions."

She grins. "I know, but watch. You'll see."

A scene materializes before us. There's a man standing over a group of people. He doesn't see us because we're not really there, or this is all some crazy hallucination. The man doesn't look like he belongs in our time or in their time. He doesn't even look like he belongs on Earth. He looms at least ten feet tall with massive fiery angelic wings and a long silver sword swathed at his side. He's dressed in a white tunic and is barefoot. His skin seems to glow, and his golden curls brush his shoulders.

Someone asks him something in a language I don't

understand. The people here are so ordinary compared to the angel, but he doesn't seem to mind. In fact, he looks down at them with nothing but unbridled love and compassion in his deep blue eyes.

"I'm a messenger of God," he says in a rich voice. There's something about his tone that is unearthly and I'm not even sure he's speaking English, but I somehow know what he's saying.

"He can be understood in all languages," Chloe whispers, sensing my confusion.

The people fall to their knees as if to worship the angel, and he commands them to stand. "My siblings and I have been directed by the Father to spread our seed over the earth. Those seeds will grow into an army meant to guide and protect the human race from the evils of the serpent."

The people erupt in prayers, questions, tears, and thanks. So many voices at once. The angel disappears with a flash of white light.

And then, once again, all I can see is white emptiness too. It's nothing, and yet it's everything, filling every space imaginable, seeping into my very soul. And then it's gone, and I'm watching time play out over the centuries, battles between the nephilim and supernaturals——all kinds of supernaturals. Werewolves. Dragons. Shifters. Fae. So many others that I've never believed in or expected or even recognize from fiction.

And vampires.

So many vampires. They multiply the fastest of all.

One by one, I witness the supernatural races fall, but the vampires are harder to kill, and they're so much stronger than the nephilim.

Generation after generation, the vampires remain.

I blink, and then I'm back in the dining room with the De Luca family.

"I think I understand now." My voice is a hoarse whisper, and my cheeks redden. How have I gotten it so wrong? Here I thought they were the bad guys, and they're the ones doing the exact thing I've been praying for all my life--ridding the earth of vampires.

Chloe releases my hand and smiles broadly.

"There is only one record keeper for our people alive at a time," Camilla says, "and we're lucky enough to have Chloe in the family." There's an undercurrent to her words, something I can't define, but it's clear how happy she is that Chloe is theirs.

I glanced over at Chloe who's now returned to her seat. "So you can travel back in time?"

"Not really travel, but I can look, and I can take other people with me to look as well."

I turn to the others. "Do you all have powers like that?" I already know Tate can manipulate people's memories and make them trust him, that Camilla can actually peer into someone's mind and riffle around as if sorting through files. I'm pretty sure Remi was trying to sway my emotions yesterday when she kept grabbing my hands. What else can these people do to me?

"Every nephilim has a special gift," Tate says. "Each gift is tied to that individual's mission here on earth."

"We're not angels, though." Greyson speaks so loudly that I nearly jump. "We're humans with some of their blood, that's all. And with every generation, we're weaker and weaker. So don't get any ideas into your head about what you can do."

"I'm not sure what ideas those would be," I shoot back.

"That's enough," Camilla cuts him off. "What matters is that Evangeline is part of the family now. This is what we do here. We find those with angelic blood, bring them in, and teach them how to protect themselves from evil, and if they choose, how to hunt that evil down and kill it."

I'm definitely interested in hunting, but this whole thing has me a little confused and unsettled. I still can't believe it's real, but then again, I can. It explains so much. "I would know if my mother was some kind of angel, and believe me, she's not." They laugh awkwardly, but I wasn't joking. "My father was killed when I was a baby," I go on. "So I must have gotten this gene from him."

"It stands to reason," Dario says dryly. I shoot him a scathing glare. What does he expect from me? This is all new, and it's not like I have any answers about my heritage. "Did you know him? He was Italian. Maybe he went to this school? His name was Carlos Russo. My mother gave me her last name."

They shake their heads, everyone claiming not to have known him. Fredrico explains, "Most with our blood will live perfectly normal human lives without ever knowing what they really are."

"But what about the gifts?" I can hardly imagine that someone with special gifts like these would not suspect something was different about them.

"Most people never live the purpose they were here to live. And if they don't live their purpose," Tate picks up the explanation, "then those gifts will never surface." He rubs his hands together. "Unfortunately, that's that."

"We can sense those who are like us, and we look for them, bringing them here when we find them. It's not enough to slow the vampiric scourge though, which is why we started recruiting the younger humans to help us with our cause," Camilla says.

I'm angry about that, but I get it. The vampires keep growing in number. It's not like these nephilim can bite someone and turn them into part-angel. It's something a person has to be born with. It would also explain why this family is large. They'd want to have as many children as they could to recruit into their little army. I'm actually surprised there aren't more of them.

"Tell them about Queen Brisa," Camilla says, her eyes gleaming with triumph. "Tell them what happened, what I saw."

I take a deep breath, not used to giving away so much information but deciding it needs to be done. "You already know she tried to turn me, and I think that's when my gift surfaced because my hands started to glow and then light exploded out. I'm pretty sure it killed her."

Adrian already confirmed it, but Camilla didn't get that far with my memories. She stopped after that moment. She takes my hand again, and all the roughness from before is gone. She's soft edges and brimming with childlike excitement. Everyone is looking at me the same way. Whatever the light thing is, they must think it's cool, and suddenly they're not so distrustful of me.

"It's the miracle we've been praying for," she says, and then everyone is talking at once.

"The blood bonds will be severed," Enzo says to Nicco. "We need to get out there!"

"She couldn't have killed her," Dario adds. "We would've heard word of it. It would be all over the news."

"They'll try and keep it a secret," Lainey says.

"There have been increased vampire attacks," her husband agrees.

"We should alert the other families," Tate says, "all nephilim need to be in on this."

"Not until we know for sure," Dario cuts him off. "We haven't confirmed."

"He's right," Lainey argues. "They deserve to know. Everyone does. The humans too."

"Enough!" Camilla bursts out, and we all turn to her. She really does know how to command respect. She accepts nothing less. "We will proceed with business as usual until we can confirm the death. But I suspect what Eva believes happened, did indeed happen because I saw it too. I didn't see her burn, the light was too bright, but it makes sense."

We talk for a while, but I'm sent to bed without most of my questions being answered. All I know is these people truly believe they were put on the earth by God to rid it of supernaturals, and they've done a pretty good job at eradicating them all except for vampires. There are families of neph all over the world who have known about this mission for generations, and the De Lucas are the oldest and wealthiest. They claim to be training others to further their cause, that they only take energy from humans that are close to death, and that they're the good guys.

But how much of that is actually true? How long until I figure out they're lying to me, too? It's hard for me to trust anyone, and I don't know if that's because I'm being smart or because my trust has been broken so many times before that I no longer know what it feels like. The information they gave me tonight is all I have to go on, so I choose to assume the others I saw stealing energy from perfectly healthy humans at the Neon club were not from this family. I'm hoping for the best here, but also preparing for the worst.

CHAPTER 17

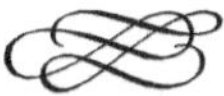

The De Lucas welcome me into their fold. The next day they introduce me to the other students and get me started with classes. We're a small group, but we spend time with the teachers and the older family members. We're here to learn everything there is to know about supernatural history and nephilim ancestry, and we work on our physical training constantly, similar to what I did back home with the hunters. And each afternoon the others go off to hone their unique gift, but the light still hasn't returned to my hands. I don't know how to get it back, and neither does anyone else.

"Everyone's gifts are as unique as the individual," Remi says to me one day when she finds me sitting in the courtyard alone. "Don't worry, yours will come back when you're ready."

I scoff. "And when will that be?"

She shrugs. "When God needs you."

All this talk of God leaves me even more confused. I still don't know what I believe or how heaven is supposed to work. And honestly? I don't think the others really know either. Not truly. They have faith—— something I've always lacked.

The sun is strong today, making this the warmest room in the house, and I've been pretending I'm back home for the last hour. Remi must see the pain in my eyes because she sits next to me, our backs to one of the huge potted plants, and gives me a small smile. "Can I help? I can make you feel better."

Normally I would say no, but today feels especially bleak, so I take her hand and she instantly floods me with a peaceful calm. I drift away on that blissed-out feeling, like a fluffy little cloud in the middle of a summer's afternoon sky. *Everything will be alright. It always is. One way or another.*

But that's not true. It wasn't for Kenton. It wasn't for my father who died when I was an infant. It wasn't for Grammy when she died of cancer in her sixties, and it wasn't for my mom when she got addicted to gambling.

I drop Remi's hand. "Sorry," I say, "I just can't lie to myself."

"It's not a lie," Remi insists. "You have access to these feelings at any time, I'm just helping you along is all."

I stand and brush myself off. "Thanks, but I know what I have to do."

Despite the vampire venom making it so much easier

to see, feel, and do whatever I want, there's one thing I've been needing that I can't get. And no, it has nothing to do with the light tucked away in my body.

I go find Camilla in her office. It's more of a sitting room, and she's there often, handling the business of running the household, her family, and more importantly, hunting down the bad guys. She peers up at me over her laptop and shuts it as I pad inside the room.

"I'd like to call home," I say, "it's really important."

I expect an argument, but she immediately hands me a cell phone. I wander into the corner of the room and dial mom's number. An answering machine tells me that the number has been disconnected. Tears well in my eyes as I return the phone to Camilla. "I haven't talked to her in almost two months," I say, my voice cracking helplessly. "This has never happened before."

"Why don't you email her?" Camilla offers, patting her computer chair. I slide onto the chair, typing out an email to my mom, letting her know I'm safe but not saying where I am, and asking her to please email me back.

"Thank you," I whisper when I finish. "I don't know what else to do."

"We'll help you look for her," Camilla responds with a grandmotherly smile. There's a warmth in her that's usually missing, and I hope I can trust it to be real. "We have a lot of resources and contacts at our disposal. We'll do our best."

I thank her and leave. I know I should feel better, but I don't.

I'm running on a treadmill a few weeks later, my mind moving faster than my feet. I keep thinking about what it would feel like to take energy from a human. I don't want to, but if I did, would it bring the light back? The longer I'm here without my gift resurfacing, the more I worry about my future. Sure, my senses are heightened, and I've grown used to it. It's like the lights have been turned on after a lifetime of living in the dark. I can see and feel and *do* so much more. And yet, there's even more waiting to be unlocked.

And it's tempting––all this power is like a drug. How easy would it be to slip into bad habits and end up hurting someone? I can't risk it, so I vow never to do so.

"I have a surprise for you, child." Camilla finds me, gliding into the gym. Her voice is a calming presence to the thumping of hip-hop music the other students like to work out to. Several of them turn to eavesdrop on our conversation.

My heart leaps. "Did you find my mother?" I've been worried sick about where she could be. So far, there haven't been any updates. I stop the treadmill and rub a towel at my hands and neck, following Camilla from the gym. My skin feels flushed and my limbs loose, which is about the only thing that feels good right now.

She doesn't answer my question, and I don't know if

that's a good thing or not. She takes my hand and leads me into the center courtyard with the greenhouse roof. New flowers bloomed recently, and it's probably my favorite place in the Casa these days. Autumn has lost its battle to winter, and I miss being outside.

Someone is waiting for me next to a row of orchids. It's not my mom standing there, but it is Felix. I haven't seen him since that horrible experience in the castle. My heart thuds, and my cheeks warm.

"I'll leave you two to talk," Camilla says, then flits from the room.

"I wondered where they took you," he says cautiously. "You look well. I see you didn't turn into a vampire after all."

"You look well, too." I smile at him because it's good to see him healthy and alive, even though he does look tired and a little rough around the edges.

He shakes his head. "Not really. We've been so busy hunting. Haven't gotten very many suckers, though."

My mouth pops open, and I take a step toward him. "I didn't know you guys were actually out hunting now." So much has changed. When we were all together, we had still been in training, and it had seemed like it would be a while until we'd be able to actually get out there and hunt. But then Tate decided we should attack the meeting at the casino, and everything went downhill from there. "I thought you would have returned home by now," I add.

"We haven't left Europe. There are a lot of vampires

here that we're trying to get under control, and then we'll go home." He shrugs like it makes perfect sense.

It's not what I want to hear. In New Orleans, the guys were only hunting on the side. School and lacrosse were still the main things in their lives. But now they're here, and I'm sure their whole semester is shot. I wonder what the Moreno parents must think of Felix's whereabouts. First, their daughter drops out of school after a few weeks of freshman year, and now their son has run off to the other side of the globe.

"Do your parents know why you're out here?"

His eyes narrow, as if considering how much he wants to say. "They think I'm studying abroad right now."

So they don't know what he's doing or they'd have dragged him home by now. That family is good at staying out of trouble. They're the sort of people I aspire to be someday, even though I accepted long ago that it will never happen. It's one thing to daydream about nursing or police work, but it's quite another to do something about it. I'm a hunted woman, and until I can get control of my neph gift, I'm stuck in the Casa.

"Listen, I'm really sorry about all the horrible things I said to you back at that castle," my voice drops.

His lips thin, and he nods. "I've had a lot of time to think about it over and I see now that none of it was you."

"It wasn't. The venom made me into a different person."

He nods once. "But what you said still hurt me, Eva." I think of how I rubbed my relationship with Adrian in his face and wince. "But I'm not mad at you anymore. I want to be your friend, but I'll never be able to try again with you." He clears his throat awkwardly. "Romantically, that is."

I don't blame him, but I'm suddenly filled with so much regret that it's physically painful. I'd kneel down and cry right now if I could, but I don't want to embarrass myself, so I reach out to offer a handshake instead. "Friends?"

"Always." We shake, and he smiles, but it doesn't quite reach his eyes. I realize I'm smiling too, and like him, my smile feels forced.

We step away from each other and begin to circle the courtyard, admiring the plants because that's easier to talk about than everything that hangs between us. I'm especially taken by the lilies. I lean down to smell one, savoring the floral scent, and notice the flower next to it as one I recognize from my studies.

"Wolfsbane," I mutter.

The plant is used to poison werewolves, but since the wolves have been hunted to extinction, there's no need for it save for its pretty lavender petals that are nice to look at.

"Maybe the family keeps it around just in case it's ever needed again?" Felix offers, and I shudder at the idea–vampires are scary enough. All I know of werewolves comes from television, and I can't imagine adding those monsters into the mix.

"So what are you on to next?" I ask.

"Seth and I have joined up with some of Tate's other hunters here. They're a good group of people. I think we'd like to stay and work with them for a while."

"How long is a while?" What I'm really wanting to ask is when is he going to go home. I want to press him on his studies again, but I don't. He must know what I'm thinking, though, because he turns me to him and squeezes my shoulders, peering down into my eyes with a serious expression.

"A while would be until I'm twenty-four if I can help it. This mission is more important than my education. You see that, right?"

But why does he have to be the one to hunt? Why does he have to give up so much of his future when most humans willingly donate their blood? Then again, now that Brisa is dead, many vampires are going to go rogue and start killing their prey. If there was ever a time to squash them, right now would be it. I'm tempted to convince him to harvest some vampire venom for himself since it will make him a better hunter, but I don't say anything because the idea of trying to extract venom is terrifying, and I know Felix would want to try. Maybe he's already working on it. Felix and Seth know a little about this stuff already, thanks to me.

"So when do you go back out?" I ask.

"Actually, for the time being, we're staying here,"

Seth's voice interrupts us, and I turn to find him striding toward us with his hands in his pockets and his hard eyes fixed on me. I can instantly tell he's still pissed off at me. He doesn't have the same forgiveness that Felix does, but I can't blame him for that. Seth and I don't have the best history, and we've only known each other since August. Not to mention, Seth is secretly in love with Felix. As far as I know, he still hasn't come out of the closet. He hates that I figured it out. It makes him uneasy around me, but his sexuality is something I'll never break his confidence on.

"I just spoke with Camilla," Seth explains, looking at Felix and not me. The lack of eye contact isn't lost on me. "They want to up their security around here, so she's asked our team to stay on for the time being."

Felix's reaction is unreadable. I can't tell if this is good or bad news when he nods and says, "Alright, then."

Is it alright?

Not to me. Sure, it's nice to see them again, but everyone here is a nephilim. I don't think they all have strong abilities or are built to be fighters, but none of them have auras, so I know they're not regular humans. And what does that mean? They'll be tempted to feed on my friends!

Right now, Felix's aura is swirling in shades of purple, and Seth's is a stormy blue, but I have no idea what those colors even mean. When I asked about aura colors during one of the lessons, I was told the others can't see them. I didn't reveal that they could if they used blacklights, but I'm sure they know all about that. Apparently, Greyson is the only one that can see them like I can, but his sight has something to do with his gift, not venom, and that guy is a Grump with a capital G.

"So we'll be seeing a lot more of you," Seth finally addresses me. "And the others like you."

I blink as his words settle in. "Wait, so you know what I am?"

They nod in unison. "Tate told us a few days before bringing us here. You've got angelic blood," Felix says. "That's pretty cool, Eva."

I bet Tate did more than just tell them about me, he probably used his Jedi-mind-tricks to make them think the nephilim are worthy of protection no matter the costs.

The conversation moves to sleeping accommodations and schedules, but I'm distracted by their swirling auras. The colors are truly magnificent. A longing burns through me, something I haven't allowed myself to feel before now. I'm like a magnet being pulled toward these men because of their energy.

I could try sucking up some of their energy, just a little bit so that nobody would know. And why shouldn't I? They are here to help us, and I think Felix would do just about anything for me. If taking a bit of his energy unlocked my gift, then he would want me to try.

"Are you even listening?" Seth asks with a dark scowl.

"You look a little pale," Felix adds. He leans down and peers into my eyes while pressing his palm to my forehead. "Are you okay?"

He's all up in my space now––that purple aura swirling around me and calling out to my base instincts. It would be so easy.

No.

I step back. "I've got to go," I sputter. "I'll see you around, okay?" Before he can respond, I take off, practically sprinting from the courtyard. My tennis shoes smack against the stone floor, and plants brush my elbows as I run past them. I can hear Seth questioning Felix about my behavior, but I don't allow myself to turn back.

It's not good that they're here. It's actually very, very bad. Because they're going to be hurt. *Used.* If not by me, then by one of the many other neph roaming these halls. Surely, the others will desire their energy the way I just did?

This is not okay.

The farther I get away from them, the more I can relax and gather myself together. I decide to steer clear of my friends, but in the meantime, I've got to get a handle on this darker side of myself because if I don't learn to control it, it will control me.

CHAPTER 18

ADRIAN

We're gathered in the palace ballroom, the garden terrace doors thrown open to let the cold air fill the space. Winter is upon us, it's a new moon, and the cloud cover is heavy. The darkness is thicker than usual, and I find myself sinking into it, letting it soothe me. I've spent so many years hiding from the sun that dark places have become a comfort zone.

I'm currently standing in one of the doorways as I observe the others mingle and find their seats. Above them, the chandeliers drip with long rivers of creamy wax from the candles Brisa had insisted replace the modern lights. Sebastian flits from group to group, his charismatic smile never once faltering as he networks through the crowd. Most of the guests are dressed in contemporary clothing, but he's still wearing the same ridiculous renaissance outfit Brisa had picked for him. It doesn't surprise me. Seb has always cared about appearing traditional, and tonight is especially important for his cause. If only he'd died with Brisa and the others, this would be so much easier.

I'm unmoving as I focus my hearing on the conversations, hoping for a sense of which vampires voted for which plan––mine and Mangus's, or Sebastian's. A few vamps are open with their opinions, but most have enough sense to keep their opinions to themselves. Tonight proves to be more of the same, though I can't say I blame anyone for skirting around the true reason we're all here. One never knows when an enemy could be plotting, and even friends can't be trusted when they have too much time on their hands. Even my own coven back home is growing restless without me. I've been in contact with them daily, but if I don't return soon, they'll find reasons to doubt my leadership.

"Are you ready for this?" Mangus slides up next to me. He's one of several who were tasked with making sure the votes were properly counted, and the man looks exhausted. If only vampires could sleep, I'd send him away for a week's worth of slumber, but perhaps the dark circles under his eyes have more to do with grief and less to do with the election.

I nod once. "The courtiers aren't going to let this go if they lose tonight," I say. "Are you prepared to fight for this, Mangus?"

He nods. "I couldn't care less about the court. At this point, they can all burn in hell. Most of them are lazy, entitled leeches."

"Tell me how you really feel."

He's right, of course. Everyone from Brisa's court has attended the meetings that we've held over the last two days. We've debated about how to proceed since her death, and the courtiers have been the most vocal about clinging to a royal system. They hate that we're putting this to a vote that includes all coven leaders. If they had it their way, they'd be the only ones who get a say. And then, of course, there are the vampires who want to break away--coven leaders who see no reason to be governed by others.

Mangus snorts. "Do you know how long I've spent pretending to like these people?" He points to a group of courtiers dressed in the same regalia as Sebastian. They're grouped up together, their noses held high.

I shoot him a hard look because, for one thing, I do know how that feels, but more importantly, he needs to keep his mouth shut. Especially now that we're so close to an uprising.

"Okay, yeah, yeah, I get it," he relents. "I'll hold on a little longer."

"There are many here I don't recognize." I nod to some of the coven leaders. They've traveled from all around the globe, a mix of ages, genders, shapes, sizes, and ethnicities. I haven't admitted it to Mangus, but the diversity has given me a measure of hope. Mangus knows many of them since he was always on the move at Brisa's bidding. His contacts have served us well throughout the debates, but it's become clear that most of the queenless court will do anything to keep their status. There's no vampire court if there's no king or queen, so they see a vampiric council as a threat, especially the ones who aren't coven leaders.

Mangus saunters off to the drinks table, snatching up an entire bottle of bloody wine. When Mangus turned out to be alive, Sebastian had been utterly floored that he'd been so wrong about everything. Mangus, on the other hand, had nearly ripped Seb's head off. Katerina is dead because Sebastian had insisted she was responsible for the princes being killed off. But everyone had gotten it wrong, and none of us have been able to figure out what really happened. It was probably hunters, but we can't know for sure, and without Brisa to investigate, we may never know the truth.

A human fledgling scurries up to me and bows low, her sheath of perfect hair shining like glass under the candlelight. She's Sebastian's, and I'm surprised he hasn't turned her by now. "The live feed is all set up," she says in a sultry voice. "We're ready to go."

"Thank you." I peel myself from the doorframe and stride to the front of the room, eyeing the camera on the tripod.

Sometimes technology amazes me, sometimes it feels

like we've always had it, and sometimes I want nothing to do with it. Tonight, I'm grateful. While many coven leaders traveled here, most had downright refused. There are over two thousand covens, and many leaders worry about their safety, refusing to venture from home. They're smart to stay back. With so many of us in one place, we're primed for an attack. But it's not hunters that worry me. Whichever way the vote goes, a lot of vampires will be unhappy.

Someone scurries forward and hands me a microphone. I tap on it, and the sound thumps through the room. I hope whatever I say will bring our kind closer together instead of splintering us further apart. The solution Mangus and I have proposed is so simple. One governing system with universal laws, covens operating as they are now, and all vampire-run businesses paying fair share in taxes and blood donations so we can keep our people healthy and a strong Vampire Enforcement Coalition tasked with enforcement. But with so many egos involved, egos who want a royal family to run things, there's a good chance none of this will happen.

And Sebastian has the biggest ego of them all.

He claims the three of us princes should take over, but I'm sure he'd just kill us and instate himself as king. I've been around long enough to know how royal families actually work.

I clear my throat as someone hands me a sealed envelope. The crowd quiets and watches in anticipation as I tear it open and read the contents, careful to keep my face a mask of indifference.

"Thank you all for being here and for your votes. We polled all the courtiers and every coven leader to come to this agreement, and we demand that you respect the outcome." Some nod their heads while others do nothing. The energy in the room grows impossibly tense. "Let it be known that a majority vote has been reached. With a vote of seventy percent, you have chosen a democratic vampiric council to replace the monarchy."

A few people voice their dissent, but many more cheer their approval. I have to fight back a grin. "The council will consist of Brisa's three remaining princes—me, and my brothers, Mangus and Sebastian. We will be joined by six other leaders representing the six continents." Vampires don't live on Antarctica, but everywhere else in the world has thousands, and the amounts are roughly the same from continent to continent. "The leaders of each continent will be voted into power by the coven leaders presiding over their respective continent. Elections will be held every ten years, and council leaders can be reelected."

"What happens if one of the princes dies?" a courtier calls out.

"If one of the princes were to perish, then the seat would remain vacant. However, if there isn't an odd number of council seats, then the council may bring in a new member but only if all council members agree on who that vampire will be."

Silence . . . because this effectively *ends* the monarchy.

"This isn't our way!" someone shouts, and then another vamp responds, "Times have changed, you old git!"

"Enough," I roar into the microphone and glare out at the crowd. "It has also been voted that if you choose to leave the protection of the council at any time, you will be hunted down by the VEC and brought before a tribunal." The room falls to silence, and several vampires send me death-glares. "The VEC is hereby instructed to enforce our laws by any means necessary."

A few more people grumble, and I drop the paper, speaking to them now as a man. "These results should come as no shock. Many have wanted to create a different system for years. We loved our queen, but she is gone now, and her royal blood bond is irreplaceable. It's time we step forward into the future. We did it eighteen years ago, and we do it again today."

I get a few cheers from that. I clear my throat and continue. "It's also been voted by a margin of sixty percent that all of Brisa's laws will stay in effect until the first council meeting, at which time they'll be voted on by your elected leaders and princes. Elections are to be held by January first, and the council's official commencement meeting will take place at an undisclosed time and location shortly after."

People start talking again, throwing names around about who should represent their continents. Most of the courtiers are European, and they're the loudest of them all. Several are standing and throwing their arms about, making claims and nominations.

"I'm not done," I roar, and the crowd reluctantly quiets. "Let it be known that anyone convicted of attempting to usurp the council and stage a coup will be given true death by way of the sun."

Silence . . . *finally.*

"That is all." I put the microphone down, and the buzz returns. I nod to Mangus in the back of the room and start toward the exit. We need to talk in private about Eva. Now that this has been taken care of, I need to get to her. Using Brisa's access to video surveillance and radar logs, Mangus was able to track her to the Italian coast. He's agreed to help me get her back. In a way, I think this has become a means for him to process what happened to his wife. He couldn't save Kat, but Eva still has a chance.

A throat clears, and I swing back to find Sebastian with the microphone. I narrow my eyes at the man who's always been a thorn in my side.

"There is one last thing that needs to be brought up before we end this proceeding," he says, voice sweeping through the crowd. They quiet for him in a way that they didn't for me and it makes me want to scream. "There's still the unfortunate matter of *how* our beloved queen lost her life."

I go utterly still. Mangus appears next to me and tugs me closer to the edge of the room. "We don't need to be the center of attention right now," he whispers under his breath, but I want nothing more than to storm up there and knock the microphone from Seb's greedy fingers.

"As some of you may know, but many do not, I was there when it happened," he goes on, pressing a hand to his chest as if the memory pains him. "It took me a week to heal my wounds, and I'm lucky to be alive. My poor prodigy was able to get me out, though, and I owe her my life."

He nods toward the pretty human woman who'd helped me earlier, then finds my gaze and smiles cruelly. "As you know, many were not so lucky as I, our beloved queen among them."

Beloved? No. Feared and respected, but never loved.

"I wouldn't have believed it if I hadn't seen it myself," he goes on. "But Brisa wasn't staked, she was burned by sunlight." Whispers erupt, and I'm seconds away from ripping the man's head off. But in such a public setting, there's nothing I can do to stop him now. "You see, Brisa was in the middle of creating a new child. Her first in centuries and the only daughter she ever wanted."

My throat goes dry. "No," I whisper and Mangus shakes his head once.

"The human girl that Brisa was attempting to change was part nephilim." More murmurs. Those with angelic blood are not always easy to spot, but I had sensed something different in Eva the moment I'd met her, and had confirmed it when I'd tasted her blood during our first kiss. It was a big part of why I chose her to spy on

Tate for me. She wasn't just another one of his human pawns, she was something more, even if she didn't know it. Of course, Brisa had confirmed everything and then tried to take Eva for herself.

Sebastian wipes a tear from his eye. An actual tear!

"Oh hell, what a load of crap," I mutter.

"It was during the middle of the ritual when blood had already been exchanged that the nephilim's hands began to glow."

I knew something would happen when she tried to turn a neph, but didn't know what exactly. My stomach hardens at Sebastian's description of the events. This is not good for Eva. It changes everything.

"Evangeline Blackwood is her name. And her angelic power replicated that of the sun. She used it to attack and kill our queen."

People are talking now. Some don't believe it, but most do. Some are afraid, but most are angry. I still don't know how to feel.

"I've never heard of such a thing," I speak up, striding toward my brother against my better judgment. Mangus winces but follows after me. "How can you be sure it was the sun?"

"Are you questioning me?" He laughs bitterly. "I'm not surprised. Ladies and gentlemen, Eva was supposed to be Adrian's child, but Brisa took her from him. He's only defending her because he wants her for himself."

I won't deny it, but I won't admit it either. "If you're mistaken, then you would be hunting down an innocent.

And how do we know that's what really happened when you were the only witness? It's her word against yours."

"My fledgling survived," he challenges. "She's a witness."

"She's your witness! She's your fledgling! We all know they'll do anything to please us."

"So you're claiming Eva is innocent? She's hardly innocent! She's a neph with the sun in her fingers, and she needs to be brought to justice."

"And she's very much alive!" Someone comes striding into the room, and I turn to find the vampire I threw into a lake instead of killing. She skips up to Sebastian and kisses his cheek. "I saw her alive, and so did you." She glares at me. I'm waiting for her to call me out on what happened that night at the castle, but she doesn't say anything. Sebastian had sent his minion after my girl, and he needs to pay for it.

"I felt her power," the woman continues, addressing the crowd. "My father speaks the truth."

"There hasn't been a light-bearer in generations," Sebastian says. "If she is what I think she is, then this could change everything." The term light-bearer presses at me like a knife. It's a legacy among the neph, and if Eva really is one, she'll never rest another day in her life. Everyone will want a piece of her. "Evangeline Blackwood is one of two things to us. She's either our greatest enemy, in need of snuffing out," the crowd likes that idea, "or she's our greatest weapon that we must possess."

"And what would you do with her?" someone calls out.

"Trust me with her and I'll give you the one thing our queen never could." His grin spreads like an ink stain. "I'll harvest her power for ourselves, and together, we will once again walk in the sunlight."

CHAPTER 19

Staying away from Felix and Seth proves to be impossible because they're swapped out for my current guards. Tate insists it's to make me feel more comfortable, but I don't believe that for a second. He's trying to tempt me into taking their energy. They sold me on this idea that they only "help" the humans who are ready to pass, but that's got to be a lie. I've reiterated that I won't do it, even on those humans who are dying, so what better way than to force it on me through sheer proximity?

If I don't give in, I'll eventually do it by accident, and I won't be able to directly blame anyone but myself. And then what? Will I be hooked on human energy? Will I want to do it more––trading one form of vampirism for another? Something terrible was unlocked within me when my hands glowed, and I want nothing more than to go back in time and undo all of this from ever happening. If only I could be like the nephilim whose gifts never emerge, living life thinking about ordinary stuff instead of worrying about sucking my friends dry. The De Luca family must really want my gift to come back, enough for them to force the issue.

"Hey, I need to talk to you guys about something in private," I whisper to Felix and Seth as we finish up dinner a week into their new assignment.

We're given free time most evenings which the three of us use to hang out in my room and watch movies. I've even tried to keep my distance from the other nephilim, but Remi keeps showing up. She's crashed most of our movie nights, so I need to take my friends somewhere she won't check right away.

"Is everything okay?" Felix's voice is brimming with concern as he slings an arm around my shoulder. He might not be so kind after I tell him the truth, and I savor the friendly gesture while I can. It was a little strained at first, but after a few days, things between us went back to how they were before we dated. It's nice to have my friend back, and I want to keep it that way.

But a week of having them as my constant companions has made this secret unbearable. A primal need is building, urging me to taste their energy. My instinct says it'll be as easy as breathing, not something I'll have to practice or study. Something that will happen the second I let the floodgates down. They deserve to know the risks.

"Not here." I feel like everywhere I go in the Casa

someone is watching me. Listening in. Waiting for the moment to strike. The De Luca family lives all over the world, but this is their home base, and Camilla called them all here only recently. They won't confess why, but from their lingering stares, I suspect it has something to do with me and my power.

"Let's go swimming," I offer. "It'll be the perfect place to talk." The weather has grown bitter over the last few weeks, turning most people off from wanting to swim in the cool pool water. If Remi comes looking for us, she probably won't check there first.

"Sure," Seth says in an agreeable tone that surprises me. The guy still hasn't warmed up to me. He's here for the job and for Felix. Not me.

I eye his blushing cheeks and fight back a smile. I know exactly why he's keen on the idea of swimming. Witnessing Felix in swim trunks is a real treat; I used to melt every time the Moreno's would take me along to the pool.

We go back to our rooms and then head down to the pool twenty minutes later. I smile at the empty room. I love being right. It's just us tonight. Nobody to pry, nobody to tattle. I slide into the cool water, and Felix cannonballs in. Seth chuckles and jumps in after him. We swim for a few minutes, and before I know it, I'm making unnecessary waves again.

"You okay there?" Seth stops me. "Is this an angel blood thing?"

I shake my head. "I actually think it's a vampire

venom thing." I quickly change the subject to why I brought them here. "I wanted to talk to you guys about something important. Something that you won't like." I swallow hard, and the three of us swim to the edge of the pool. I lean against the side and let my legs drift up. I can't bring myself to look them in the eye, so I gaze off toward the closed door.

"So what is it?" Seth prods.

Now or never. "Do you remember the energy demon things? I know we talked about this before, but then Tate tampered with things, so I'm not really sure--"

"The what?" Felix questions.

"The energy demons?"

They stare at me, and I get the confirmation I need. Tate really did clear so much from their minds.

"Let me back up and explain," I say timidly. "Cameron Scout was the first one to alert me to them. They're people who steal energy from human auras, similar to how vampires take our blood."

"Auras?" Seth questions. "You mean the energy color things people are supposed to have around them? I didn't think those were real."

Felix's lips twist as he ponders.

"Okay, let me explain." I swim out to the middle of the pool and turn on them, "Auras are real, people can even take pictures of them, so let's not try to contest that, okay? An aura is like this energy field of color around a human. They change throughout the day depending on what's going on with someone, but the core colors tend to stay the same." I swallow hard, afraid I'm going to lose them. "Long story short, supernaturals don't have auras, and neither do the nephilim." I shrug. "I don't have one. I thought it was just that I couldn't see my own, but it turns out that it's because of the whole neph thing."

"You can see these auras?" Felix's eyes widen. I've got him curious. "Can you see mine right now?"

"If I think about it, yes, I can."

"What color is it?"

"Right now? Mainly blue. But that's not the point," I rush on. "Just let me explain. It turns out that nephilim can take energy from these auras."

Seth frowns. He's not sure about all this.

"I promise, they can. They do it to strengthen their gifts, but when they do it, it hurts the human."

"Have you done it?" Seth asks.

"No, not yet, and I don't want to, but there's this voice inside screaming at me to try. This is why I wanted to bring you somewhere private to talk. I think Tate brought you here to tempt me. He wants me to get a taste of your energies."

Felix shakes his head. "No, Tate wouldn't do anything to hurt us."

"He's right. Tate is on our side."

I scoff. "Are you kidding me? You're in constant danger because of him. Why do you trust someone who--"

"You're wrong," Seth's interruption is harsh. "We

don't have anything to worry about, and you shouldn't either."

"Come on, let's go. It's getting too cold in here anyway," Felix sounds almost robotic, but sure enough, they climb out of the pool, going for the towels like our conversation didn't happen.

They shift from being stiff and defensive to relaxed and their normal selves in a matter of seconds, then turn to wait for me. I'm flabbergasted, and anger burns through me as realization dawns. Of course, this was always going to happen. I should've realized it sooner. Tate has used his memory manipulation and persuasion ability on my friends as he's done time and time again. They're never going to believe me. And if they do, it won't be long until he's back, whispering things in their ears.

As I climb from the pool, tears splash down my cheeks, mixing with the pool water. Nobody says a word. And then I'm struck with a heartbreaking thought––do they actually care about me? When they first came here, they didn't seem all that happy to see me, especially not Seth. Their forgiveness came quickly and easily. What if everything has been against their free will? Suddenly, their friendship feels like another one of Tate's lies. They're here because of him, not because of me, and I have no idea how to make it stop.

CHAPTER 20

"We have a surprise for you," Remi beams, taking my hand and leading me outside after dinner.

It's officially been three weeks since I arrived at the Casa, and I'm no closer to figuring out how to access my power, let alone finding my mom or helping my human friends break free of Tate's hold. I'm caught in an endless loop, waiting for something to happen, and I can't keep up the charade much longer.

Warm happiness pulses through me with the squeeze of her hand, and I push the emotion away. She frowns. "I just want to help you to relax. You've been so uptight lately, Eva."

I drop her hand and sigh, gazing up at the night sky sprinkled with stars, but the winter wind whips my hair back and brandishes my skin with goosebumps. Even though I'm wearing a coat, it's not enough to combat the cold. The burn of venom is still strong but I only enjoyed the cold during those three awful days and nights. I fight the urge to tell Remi off and run back inside. "I know you do, and while I appreciate you wanting to help me feel more comfortable, I need to be the one in charge of my emotions."

"Alright, I get that." She sounds dejected.

"What's the surprise?" I try to make my voice honey-sweet, but I'm pretty sure it comes out as bitter as vinegar. "I promise I'm excited," I go on, "I'm just not used to this cold and I'm being a baby about it."

That, and she's right, I *am* uptight. Who wouldn't be in this situation?

"It will be worth the crappy weather, I promise." She grins and turns to motion Felix and Seth closer. They're always nearby since guarding me is their job now, and I hate that I can't call Tate out on it. Not yet anyway. But soon enough, I will. I just have to find leverage first, a reason to get him to do what I want. There's got to be something I can use against Tate. Nobody's innocent, and I'm sure Tate has more secrets than most in this house.

Remi leads us out on the big lawn in the back of the Casa where a crowd is gathering. All the students and most of the household staff mingle in tight-knit groups, all dressed in lush winter attire. There are generations of wealth here, and I'd stick out like a sore thumb if it weren't for the fact that Camilla had my closet outfitted with the same luxurious clothing. Tonight, I'm dressed in thick tights, a soft camel-colored cable-knit sweater dress, matching boots, and a black peacoat. My outfit isn't half as extravagant as my peers' but I feel more put together than I ever used to back home.

Gentry gives our group a little wave, his eyes landing on Seth and a dimpled smile lighting his face. He's with his crew, and Bella swats his arm down, hissing something I can't hear. There are not many students here, but most seem indifferent to my presence, and the De Luca family is a mixed bag of kindness and distrust. Besides Remi, Gentry is the nicest person I've met, and Bella and her brother Greyson are the worst.

"Are you ready for this?" Remi giggles, pointing back to the Casa. Just as she does, the entire building lights up with twinkling gold holiday lights. Everyone cheers, and I admit it makes me smile too. It's beautiful. Orchestra music starts playing over outdoor speakers, and something else lights up behind me––a towering Christmas tree, glittering with red and green ornaments, and more gold lights.

"Wow, this is amazing," I gush, filled with awe and longing all at once.

"Isn't it?" She squeezes my hand. "Camilla loves the holidays and decorates to the nines every year."

Sure enough, the crowd splits, and Camilla stands at the base of the tree. Her family goes to her first, offering congratulations and kisses. I don't want to be rude, so I follow Remi over. Truth be told, I've avoided Camilla as often as possible except for getting help with my mom's whereabouts. Ever since that woman peered into my mind and sifted through my memories, it's hard to want to be around her. Great hospitality only goes so far when you're sure you're being manipulated. I've tried to trust everything they're teaching me here, to lean into this new role in my life, but it's been hard. I still have my walls up.

"How are you enjoying your time here?" Camilla asks after I compliment her on her beautiful decorating.

"It's been great," I say, not trusting her with the truth that I'm still bothered by a lot of things. "Thanks again for allowing me to stay here."

Her eyes slide over my face and a bit of that kindness dissolves into a sharp stare, confirming my intuition about her. "I've been following your progress. No light has come back into your hands, not even when you're on your own? Or perhaps by accident?"

I shake my head. "Sorry to disappoint."

"You know what you need to do, do you not?" Her eyes flick to where Felix and Seth are standing, and my stomach hardens.

"If you're asking me to hurt anyone, I won't do it." I fold my arms over my chest and glare. "Besides, you insisted that you only take from those who are already terminal. Are you telling me that was a lie?"

Her face hardens. "That's how we usually replenish our energy stores, but every once in a while we do what's necessary. Humans are far more resilient that you might think, Eva. They bounce back quickly. A little siphoned energy here and there hardly hurts them. And wouldn't you agree that the good of humanity outweighs the experience of a few individuals?"

My stomach twists. So they were lying.

"Anyway, dear, nobody is going to make you do it." She tilts her head and smiles sweetly. "But if you would like a lesson, I'd be happy to be of service. We could even take you to the local hospital. In fact, Greyson is going tomorrow, I'm sure he'd show you the ropes."

I shake my head and stomp away, perhaps making an ass of myself, and definitely being rude to the hostess, but I don't care. Cat's out of the bag––they want my power and want me to be willing to do whatever it takes to get it, even going against their own supposed code of ethics.

"You think you're better than us?" I turn to find Tate's bratty children glowering at me. Bella is full-on glaring, and of course it's Greyson standing there with his typical judgmental sneer. His hands are stuffed into his pockets, and his black curls hang around sunken cheeks. Something about him isn't right, and I realize he might be ill. Maybe that's why he's going to the hospital tomorrow and the others aren't. There's more going on with him than anyone has let on, and I want to figure out what it is.

"I don't think I'm better than anyone," I reply. "But I'm nobody's pawn either."

Bella's laugh is bitter. "Everyone is a pawn, but that's the point. Don't you get that? We work together to win the bigger game, and the sooner you do your part to help out, the sooner--"

"Let's go," Greyson interrupts, his eyes zeroing in on his sister. "Eva's not going to change her mind."

He grabs her and drags her away to their father across the lawn, who whispers something harsh into her ear by the way she stiffens. All three turn to look at me, and I force myself to continue inside. I'm so angry, I could scream. I open and close my fists, something warm tingling between my fingers.

Light. It streams from my fingertips like golden laser beams. I squeal, and then it flashes to darkness seconds later. I almost run back out to tell Camilla, but I don't. She doesn't deserve to know.

"Woah, what's wrong with you?" Felix stops me, and Seth's mouth flattens into a thin line. I quickly close my hands and open them again, but the light is still gone. I don't have control over it, but my heart is bursting with excitement.

"I did it," I breathe out, hardly believing it myself. "You saw that, right?"

"Oh, we saw that," Seth says. He blinks, almost like he's coming out of a stupor. "This place is something else, isn't it?"

"This is what I've been trying to tell you." I widen my eyes at them. "I don't think you guys are here by your own free will and choice. I don't think it's safe for you."

Blank faces--*once again* I'm met with blank faces. I want to scream, but I force a steadying breath instead.

Both of their auras have grown brighter and larger, a mix of colors swirling around the three of us.

"If you feed on the energy, you will be more powerful." Chloe appears next to me, seemingly out of nowhere. I jump and turn on her.

"I'm not going to do that," I rush out. Felix and Seth look on, confused.

"You sure? There's ways we can do it that doesn't cause much harm. I can show you how."

"No," I insist.

"I understand where you're coming from." She twists her lips and nods toward my hands. "But I saw that too, you know. That's a good sign."

"What does it mean?"

But she doesn't say. Her face falls, a flash of concern in her eyes, and then she scrambles off before I can get another question in. I make a mental note to look for her tomorrow and demand answers, but the next day comes, and Chloe is nowhere to be found. And when I ask after her, nobody will tell me a thing.

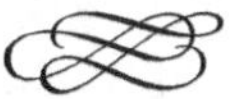

We're finishing a decadent Christmas dinner, and I'm grateful to be safe, but I'm sick with worry for my mom and friends, and in the back of my mind I know vampires are out there looking for me. I'm tired of living like this, days spent exercising, trying to find ways to pass the time, with most of the lessons being interesting but not all that helpful. The holidays have deepened my homesickness, and I'm ready for things to be different.

"Merry Christmas," Camilla calls down the long dining table, raising her glass. We all raise ours in kind, saying cheers to new year's wishes coming true. The bubbly champagne does nothing to lift my spirits.

"Now, are you ready for your gift?" Camilla continues, her eyes sparkling with yuletide mischief. "We've arranged to leave the Casa and travel to a party tonight." The room erupts into excited whispers, and I have no idea what this could mean, but I'll admit my curiosity is piqued.

I can hardly eat a bite as my stomach twists in knots. Everyone else must feel the same way because a lot of half-eaten meals are left behind as we flounce off to get ready for the party and congregate at the front of the house. It's a semi-formal event, and I've chosen an emerald green velour gown that hugs my curves perfectly but still covers me enough to keep me warm. The family stylist piled my hair atop my head, and went extra smoky with the makeup. I feel beautiful as I slip into one of the SUVs waiting in the drive and hope the party can cheer me up.

The second we leave the Casa gates behind, I breathe a sigh of relief. I'm acutely aware that I should be feeling the opposite. We're leaving the safety of the family estate *in the dark*, but I can't help but feel better. I know I'm not a prisoner, but sometimes it feels that way, and the cabin fever has been bad lately.

The roads are windy and steep, bordered on either side by beautiful Italian homes all lit up and sea-weathered stone walls shadowed by lush greenery. Even on a dark winter's night, this city is gorgeous. I'm hit with a pang of longing in my chest, a need to explore the world, to experience more than I've been allowed.

We pull up to a large ornate burnt-orange building with a stream of stylish cars already parked in the drive. Ivy climbs up one side, and lights flicker from the many windows. It's warm and welcoming, and I can't wait to get inside. Climbing from the SUV, I spot Remi and hurry over to her, Felix and Seth on my heels.

"What kind of party is this?" I ask. "Is there going to be dancing?"

Her smile falters, and my heart falls. There's something more going on here, something she knows I'm not going to like. "You'll see," is all she says, and then we're ushered up the stone steps and into the warm building.

There are humans everywhere, all immaculately dressed, partying in a huge ballroom. My fingers itch, and my heart thuds as I take it all in. Everyone is so stylish, milling about with champagne flutes in their hands as if they haven't a care in the world. A few rosy-cheeked children are running amok between the adults, most likely high on Christmas cheer and sugar. A string orchestra is set up in the far corner, and couples are dancing nearby. A buffet that could feed an army sits opposite the orchestra. And everything is tied together with decorations of green and red. I catch the scent of pine trees and sugar cookies, and breathe it in deeply, savoring the moment.

The others don't hold back. They join the party seamlessly, mixing with the humans, many of them talking like they're old friends. I stand back to survey the auras. Everyone is practically glowing, they're so happy, so vibrant, so alive. I don't think I've ever seen so many people in one place. And then the colors begin to shift and change as the nephilim feed.

"I'm sorry. This is just the way it's done," Remi says,

still at my side and practically reading my mind. Seth and Felix are a few paces off, but I'm sure they can hear our conversation. I'm not sure it will matter.

"Camilla lied to me." I clear my throat, my cheeks going hot. "Tate lied to me. They all did."

"If it's any consolation, they weren't totally lying. We don't normally do things this way," Remi continues.

"It's not," I huff.

Chloe floats up next to us. She came back on Christmas Eve from wherever she was, but I haven't had a chance to talk to her yet. "Good to have you back," I say. "Where did you go?"

She shrugs. "I had an assignment for my grandmother. No big deal."

"You left Italy?"

Her eyes flash and she laughs. "You're nosy tonight. If you must know, I was in New York City. Some of our friends needed my help with new recruits."

I can only imagine what that means.

Of all the De Luca grandchildren, Chloe's my favorite, but I still can't trust her as far as I can throw her. She turns her button-lipped smile on me. "But like I told you before I left, I can teach you ways of feeding on the humans' energy that won't hurt them that bad."

Remi goes red and looks away, which only confirms what I already think.

"Does it hurt them or not? Because hurting someone innocent without their consent is still messed up."

Chloe frowns, but doesn't say anything more, and

that's all the answer I need. She may have found some tricks, but the fact still remains that they're stealing the life-force right out of people to help fuel themselves.

And part of me longs to do the same.

Fists clenched, I march over to Camilla, ready to give her a piece of my mind, when Tate intercepts me. He grabs me by the elbow and pulls me to the edge of the party. "This was all for you. Don't look so ungrateful," he hisses.

"I never asked for this," I snap back.

"If you don't feed soon, do you know what's going to happen to you?"

"Guess I'll find out, because I'm never going to feed." I rip my arm from his grasp.

He mutters something in Italian before locking me in with his stare. His whole demeanor has changed--gone is the charismatic father figure that I'd so foolishly trusted. A manipulative liar stands over me, but I refuse to shrink or back down.

"You need to build your strength and get control of your power. Don't you want to do as God intended?"

"Oh, so you have proof that God intended for me to hurt people?" I glare, throwing up my hands. "News flash, Leslie, I don't see God anywhere around here."

"The humans hardly notice their energy leaving them, and they have more than enough to spare. And what we're doing by ridding the world of evil? It's for them."

I motion to the crowd, raising an eyebrow. The

energy in the room has started to shift, and already the merriment is being siphoned away. The nephilim are sure getting their fill, though; they look great. "You're not going to convince me."

He bares his teeth. "If I could make you do it, I would. But I can't, so I'll continue to give you opportunity after opportunity until eventually your body wears down enough for you to feed. Don't you see, Eva? You need this. You need the energy, the fuel for your gift. And you have no idea what you're missing."

"Stop lying to me, then." That gets his attention. He goes eerily still as I continue, "Why can't I get ahold of my mother?"

He blinks, startled by my sudden change in conversation. "We're not lying about that," he says defiantly. "We don't know where she is. Believe me, if we did, you'd be the first to know." There's an undercurrent of threat to his tone that sets me on edge. Goosebumps prickle across my flesh.

"What's all this about?" Dario De Luca appears next to us, oozing his typical sliminess. There's something about him that sets me the most on edge, even more so than what I feel around Tate and Camilla. Fortunately, he's kept his distance since our first introduction, but now he's standing too close with probing questions in his gaze. He pats Tate on the back. "What? Is my mother putting pressure on you to get your newest acquisition in line?" He chuckles low.

Tate brushes him off and shoots me another scathing

look. "Don't forget, you need our help. Do as you are asked or find someone else to keep you alive."

He stalks off, and Dario laughs again. His stare is just as cold as the others, and his creep factor hasn't eased in the slightest, but at least he's upfront about his feelings toward me. It's obvious he'd rather see me dead than in the Casa. He's never once smiled at me or pretended to want me around, and the few times we do make eye contact, his are glaring daggers. It's so strange that many of these people hate me, and I still haven't figured out why.

"Tell me, Eva, have you learned about the angelic-factions yet?" He takes a casual sip of his champagne.

"Factions?" This is news.

"Figures," he snorts. "Okay, let me be the one to clue you in. We nephilim aren't the most agreeable bunch. We fight amongst ourselves almost as much as we fight the supernaturals. Ironic, isn't it?"

My mouth pops open.

"Nothing to say?" He takes another long swig of his drink. "And you *just so happened* to be picked up by the most powerful faction in Europe, and I'd argue the most powerful in the world, though, some other factions would disagree."

The way he said "just so happened" makes it sound like it was anything but a coincidence. "Why are you telling me this?"

"Because the truth is, if you don't get in line here, my mother will send you off to one of our allied families to be dealt with, and let me tell you, none of them are going to put you up in a nice house, educate you, and take you to parties." He raises his glass out to the people around us, and my eyes land on Seth and Felix. They're dancing with a couple of others, no longer worried about me. "Your gift will be *forced* out, and while my brother-in-law is a brown-nosing pain in my ass, he's also right." He steers me into the crowd, hand firmly on my back. "Now, be a good little girl and do as you're told, or we'll stop asking nicely."

"Did you ever stop to think that maybe the reason your factions fight is because you're doing something wrong here? Maybe the power is corrupting you."

That makes him laugh. "You could be right, but it doesn't change anything."

Felix turns from his dance partner, and Dario shoves me into his arms. Felix's eyes are glossy as my childhood crush looks down at me, his mouth slack. He leads me in a dance, oblivious to what's really going on here. Tears prick at my eyes, and an inferno burns in my chest. I don't want to do this, any of it, and they're going to make me do it to one of my oldest friends.

I can't.

I rip away from Felix and fall into the arms of a human I don't recognize. The handsome man smiles ruefully down at me and begins speaking in Italian. I tell him I don't understand, and he laughs, but continues to speak so quickly it all blends together. His grip on me is tight as he spins me across the dance floor. I grow dizzy, my chest burning with a primal need to feed on him. His turquoise aura surrounds me, and I can feel the electric pulse of it tickling my senses. I don't want this, I don't, I don't . . . but I do. And before I can stop myself, I'm letting the turquoise flood me, like diving into the sea. The energy fills me up quickly, endorphins bursting with exuberance and life.

I want more, but my guilt is instant, and I rip away from the young man, rushing from the ballroom.

Someone laughs as I go, but I don't look to see who. It doesn't matter. They won. I did it. I did it, and it felt amazing, and I hate myself for it. I may not be a vampire, but I've become just like the very monsters I hate the most. And still, even now, the longing to go take more of that sparkly turquoise energy is stronger than ever. It whispers assurances that I'll eventually go back for more.

I search for an exit, needing fresh air, to be alone, but I can't find one that isn't surrounded by people, so I run to a stairwell instead, climbing up, up, up. My legs don't burn like they used to before everything happened. I'm so full of venom and that energy that I don't know if I'll ever feel pain again, save for my own hurt pride. I slam through a door and stumble out onto a bare rooftop. The cool air is instant salvation, and I lap it in, praying it will calm my nerves.

I drop my head between my knees, panting, crying, about to scream. What have I done?

CHAPTER 22

ADRIAN

For weeks I've been trying to get her back, and now here she is, a goddess with the warm light of the opened door illuminating her silhouette. I swallow hard at the stark thought that she's the most gorgeous creature I've ever seen, that I'd kneel down and worship her right now if I could. And then she doubles over, a cry strangling her body, and I'm frozen. I don't know what to do--I *never* don't know what to do.

She can't see me, and I want nothing more than to go to her. I don't. I stay hidden in the shadows, watching. Waiting. The door slams, light disappearing, and then I can see all of her. Her cheeks are wet with tears, and she's clenching her chest like she's been shattered and is clinging onto the broken pieces. I've never seen her like this. I'm momentarily stunned.

The desire to save her slams through me. I could

grab her and leave, even if she fights me. It wouldn't be easy, but I'd do it for her. To get her away from these people who are clearly using her--harming her. But I know Eva too well. She'd fight me every step of the way, and I need her to come with me willingly.

In the time it took me to find out where she was and get to her, I realized that taking her against her will won't give me the results I want. She needs to trust me--to believe me. She'll never do either if I force her.

She strides to the edge of the roof and stares out over the city. We're five stories up, and the vast lawn below sweeps out to the glittering lights of more buildings and then the darkness of the sea beyond. I wish I could go there with her. Take her someplace where there's nobody but us for miles. I rather like the ocean at night with its high tides and pounding waves. It doesn't scare me like it did when I was a boy. Would it frighten her? Or would she find solace in it like I do? We could find a secluded beach, lay in the cool sand and watch the clouds roll by, waiting for a glimpse of the stars, and then we could fly away.

She breaks out in a sob and it's like being shaken awake. I can't wait any longer. This may be my only chance to get her alone.

I step from the shadows, making sure my shoes rub against the concrete. She turns and gasps, eyes wide and face full of surprise. And then it falls and anger takes over. "Adrian," she says coolly, "what are you doing here?"

"I came to give you something."

She extends her hand, her features going hard, but I can hear the thumping of her heart as it accelerates. Her blood is hot and ready for the taking, but that's no longer what I want from her. "Hand it over then."

I cock my head. "So that's it, then?" I say cockily. "You're not going to ask me how I've been? No catching up for old time's sake?"

She narrows her eyes. "I think we're past fake pleasantries. If you're not here to kill me, then give me whatever it is you want to give me and leave."

"Don't you want to know about the vampires? Aren't you curious what's happened since you ran off with *them?*"

"Them?" she scoffs. "You mean the nephilim--of which you failed to tell me I was one of?"

"Brisa forbade us to speak of them or I would've told you." I step closer, and she steps back, the push and pull between us tugs at unseen wounds. But what was I expecting? She hates me, as she should. I hurt her. I made things so much worse for her. Omitted the truth. Lied at times.

She hates me.

"Fine. Whatever," she says. "I know the truth now. They've told me all about it. I've even been taking lessons."

I laugh bitterly. "Lessons, huh? You can't trust them or their lessons." To see her defend them so readily sets me off my axis. I wasn't expecting this, and now I'm spiraling out of control, seconds away from making her leave with me, the plan be damned.

"At least they told me what I am."

"I hardly doubt they told you everything you need to know." I stride to her in two long steps, no longer able to keep my distance. I pull her up against me and she yelps, but doesn't push me away. Our bodies are flush, and her intoxicating scent calls to me like a drug. "Come with me, and I'll tell you everything," I promise. "I'll answer any question, every question. Anything at all."

"No more secrets?" Her mouth parts, and I'm distracted by her blushing lips. I need to kiss her.

"No more secrets." I lean down to taste my angel, slowly so she has time to meet me halfway.

She shoves me back. Her strength has grown tenfold, and it sends me flying back. I catch myself and raise my hands in surrender. She's glaring daggers at me now, her face drawn in anger.

"Please," I growl. "Don't make me beg." A stab at my pride because I know I'll do it.

"I'll never trust you again, but I'm not stupid enough to trust the neph either. I don't think I'll trust another soul on this earth ever again, come to think of it. You should know me better than that, Adrian."

She's right. I should. *I do.* And it's my fault she's turning out this way. Me and my kind have done this to her.

I slip the little burner phone from my pocket and hold it out to her. She eyes it skeptically. "This isn't a trick. Take the phone. Call your mother. She knows the truth. She knows everything."

Her stoic mask slips, and the worry she's been harboring mars her pretty face. Part of me feels guilty for using Eva's love for her mother against her like this. She's already been through so much with that woman. But the other part of me knows this will work. If I can't get through to her, Virginia can.

"Let me guess, they can't find her?" I prod. "They've been trying for weeks, but she's nowhere to be found?"

She shakes her head and snatches the phone from my hand. Her voice cracks, "Thank you for finding her."

"You really don't get it, do you?" I say. "I didn't find her, Eva. I've been hiding her, keeping her safe."

"What?" Her mouth falls open.

"Right before we left for New Orleans she came to me, asking for my protection. I gave it to her," I shrug. "I should've told you before. It wasn't your fault you had to come to Versailles with me. I've made sure to keep your mom safe and your apartment rent paid. As for your job, that was a little trickier, but it's promised to you if you're ever able to return."

I don't have the heart to tell her things will never go back to what they were before. Now that Sebastian has every vampire in the world after her, Eva's chances at a normal life are all but decimated. But I'm holding onto her old life for her anyway, just in case. "Call her," I urge. "Call her when you're alone. Don't let anyone know you have that phone. And then call me. My number's in there too."

I hope it will be enough. And I hope she calls soon, because it's only a matter of time before the others track her here, and when that happens, I don't think the nephilim have enough precautions in the world to protect her. She's too valuable. The other vampires think they can use her ability to somehow get us back in the sun. It's enough to make the vampires do anything to get her, even attack one of our enemy's strongholds.

Before she can answer, I slip away, stepping off the edge of the roof and floating down to the lawn. I walk out into the quiet street, my mind a whirl at what just happened and my heart screaming at me to go back to her. I forgot I had a heart, to be honest, but here I am, willing to trade anything––even the sun––for that woman.

But I must be patient. I've waited this long, haven't I? What's a few more days? Hell, she may even be calling me in a few hours. My number is one of the three programmed into that phone. And I'm not scared of their compound. I'll get her out of there one way or another. And then we'll go––

Something grabs me from all sides. Seering white-hot fire sizzles my flesh as silver ropes wrap around my entire body. I grapple for an escape, but they're heavy, and when I push on them they burn even harder. I blink against the netting, realizing what's happening. I drop to my knees and try to dig, but the street is solid frozen concrete, and my muscles are growing weak.

This can't be happening . . .

This . . .

"I thought perhaps you'd follow her here," a man says, and I blink up to see my nemesis, Leslie Tate, boasting over me. "Glad to see I was right."

"What do you want?" I gasp up at the man I've been hunting for the better part of three decades. He did me wrong, killing the last prodigy I had before Kelli, and I've been trying to enact my revenge ever since but he's kept himself well-protected. The irony that he's the one who's caught me isn't lost on me. I'm so angry I want to scream obscenities, but I don't have the strength. The silver even burns through my clothes, and the searing pain is so intense I can hardly breathe, let alone scream.

No answer.

The question dies off as my body succumbs, a darkness thicker than I've known taking me out to sea.

CHAPTER 23

I stay up there for a few minutes, holding the phone in an iron-tight grip. Screw what Adrian said about waiting to call her, this is my lifeline, and I'm going to use it while I have the chance. The phone is one of those cheap burners, and I flip it open, finding three contacts listed––Virginia, Adrian, and one cryptically titled "*In Case of Emergency.*"

The phone is fully charged, but I don't know enough about these kinds of phones to gauge how long I have before it dies. Could be days or hours, and I'm not in the habit of being patient. I click on all three contacts and commit the numbers to memory. It's surprisingly easy. I never had this kind of mental aptitude before the venom, and I'm thrilled with the results.

I toggle to my mom's contact and tap the call button. She answers on the first ring.

"Evangeline, is that you?" Her voice is more panicked

than I've ever heard before, and my heart drops to my stomach.

"Yes," I gush, instantly in tears again. "It's me."

"Oh, thank God," her accent comes out thicker than usual through the tears that are surely rolling down her face. "I was so worried. Are you okay? Where are you?"

I turn around to face the door of the building, surveying the rooftop. I'm still alone out here. Edging as far from the door as I can, I start to whisper. "I'm in Italy. I'm staying with some people here who are keeping me safe from the vampires." I don't tell her that I'm okay because I don't have it in me to lie. I'm far from okay, but she sounds frantic, and I don't need to make it worse.

"What people in Italy?" she presses, voice dropping an octave.

"Didn't Adrian tell you?"

"I haven't talked to Adrian in weeks. He got me out in time and found me a safe place to hide out."

"Hide from what? What's going on, Mom? What aren't you telling me?"

She's quiet for a long moment. "Your father didn't die in a car accident, honey. He was murdered."

If the ground opened up and swallowed me whole, I'd be less surprised than this. "What?" I squeak out. My heartbeat pounds in my ears.

Her confession crashes over me like a tidal wave. I've never known much about my dad because it hurt her too much to talk about, but the one thing I did know for sure was that my father was killed in a car accident when I was a baby. "It wasn't safe to tell you," she continues. "The only one who knew the whole story was Gram."

"What's the story, Mom? Tell me!" My face is burning, and my body is floating. I'm about to drift away.

"Listen carefully," she says, growing serious. "When I met him, he told me his family was mafia and he'd gotten out, that he'd come to America because he wanted a fresh start away from all that. I fell hard for him, and I believed him, but he wasn't the man he said he was. He wasn't a bad man, but he wasn't mafia either."

"This doesn't make any sense. Why would someone lie about something like that?"

And then my mind catches on that word, and I think of my conversation with Tate that first day in his car.

"Because his family may as well have been the mafia for all the things they were mixed up in and all the pressure they put on him to carry on their legacy," she says bitterly. "They're nephilim, honey. Do you know what that means? It means they have angelic blood. I know it sounds crazy, but it's not. And you're a nephilim too, baby. He only ever told me the truth because I got pregnant and he wanted me to know what I was getting myself into with you."

"So all this time, you knew and you said nothing?" My heart drops.

"We wanted to protect you from it," she rushes on,

"and it wouldn't have affected you until you got older when I thought I'd have him there to guide you through everything. When he died, my mother got a special talisman made. She gave it to you when we feared you'd come of age soon. It was meant to keep you from ever knowing what you are and from them ever finding you."

"The necklace?" It's back in a safe somewhere in Adrian's suite. I haven't worn it since I left the country. "I figured out what it was, but not what it was supposed to protect me from." I never would've guessed.

"The witch she bought it from asked for a great price," Mom continues. "Something money couldn't buy."

Fear settles through me. "Just tell me."

"Gram's cancer wasn't just cancer," her voice cracks. "The witch got the last twenty years of her life in exchange for that talisman."

My heart sinks. And to think, I don't even have the necklace anymore. Her and Gram always insisted I wear it, and I usually did, but I didn't even fight Adrian when he took it away from me. Because it was shaped like a cross and would offend Brisa, I'd given up the protection. Did Adrian know what it really was?

"The crossing feathers on the back of the crucifix? Is that the talisman?"

"Yes," Mom continues. "It was magicked by the witch. But that doesn't matter now. What matters is you need to know the truth. You need to be safe."

"I don't necessarily like it here, but I'm pretty sure

I'm safe. I don't want you to worry about me. I want you to worry about your own safety."

"I'm fine. But, honey, remember what I said about your father being murdered?"

"It was vampires wasn't it?" This time, my voice cracks. Another thing vampires took away from me.

"No," she replies. "It wasn't vampires. It was nephilim. I don't know a whole lot about them, but I do know most of them are bad. And his family were the worst of them all." She goes quiet for a minute, and I stand still, lost and frightened and missing my mom. "Honey, your father had a unique gift, and when he refused to use it any longer, his own family had him killed."

"What?" My mind spins. "What gift? Why kill him over something like that?"

"Because sometimes these gifts can only go to one person at a time. One dies with it and another is born with it."

My voice starts to shake, fear at what this gift could be. "Tell me. What was his gift?"

She sighs heavily. "Something to do with memory."

My head spins. I don't know what any of this means. "Mom, this sounds crazy. Are you sure he was murdered? Did you see it?"

"In a way," her voice is thick with tears. "It was a car, but it wasn't an accident. I was there, honey. He saved me, and then he held my hands as he was dying and took me to this place where he could show me the past."

Realization dawns on me, and my stomach twists. "Like––he took your hands and showed you the memories? Was it a white room, and then it was like you were standing there watching something happen in real time?"

"Yes, it was exactly like that."

I swallow hard, and my fingers go numb. I'm holding the phone too tight. "Oh no," I whisper slowly, dread building in my chest. "Mom, one of the people I'm staying with can do that exact same thing. They call her the record keeper." I think of beautiful Chloe. She's about my age, but almost a year younger. Could she have been born soon after my father passed away? Was she given his ability because he refused it?

I don't want to believe it, but it must be true.

"Who are you with?" Mom presses. "What are their names?"

"De Luca."

But that's not my father's last name . . .

So was it simply fate that Chloe was the one who got my father's ability when he died? Maybe it goes to the next nephilim child to be born, and she was that one. But then why have him killed for not helping? The way I see it, someone on the brink of childbirth could have had my dad killed with the hope that their son or daughter would get the record keeper gift next. Is that something the De Luca family would do? Would they kill their own son––my father––just to get their hands on this gift and keep it within their bloodline?

I get the answer with the sound of deafening silence on the other end of the phone. Mom's panic is palpable, and fear slices through me like a hot knife. "Mom––" I press on, "don't tell me it's the same family."

I'm staring out into the darkness, watching the lights twinkle from the city below. They blur behind my eyes, and my knees go weak. I need to sit down.

"We gave you a fake name," she whispers. "Your father was the oldest De Luca son, and he insisted we change our names, that we start fresh." All at once, she erupts. No more whispering, she's screaming. "You have to get out of there! Get away from them! They'll hurt you! They'll––"

Hands push me from behind. My waist hits the edge of the railing, but I'm not fast enough to catch myself. I careen over the edge, phone flying from my grip. And then I'm falling. So fast. The night swallowing me whole, and the ground reaching up to grant me death.

CHAPTER 24

The impact never comes. I'm hovering a few feet off the ground, levitating like a certain blood-sucking vamp . . .

A stunned second after I realize what's happening, I lose control and plummet the rest of the way, hitting the ground with a smack. I groan, roll over, and sit up, frowning at the broken cell phone parts scattered around me. Thank heavens I memorized those numbers, but now I don't have a way to call anyone, and Mom has to be more worried than ever.

But at least I know the truth.

I peer up at the rooftop, searching for whoever just tried to kill me, but of course there's nothing to see but empty skyline and winking stars. I could try levitating up there, maybe catch whoever it was on their way down the stairs, but there's no chance I'm going to attempt to levitate again so quickly, and they're probably long gone. The best thing I can do is rejoin the party and see if anyone acts surprised to see me alive.

And then I have to figure out how to get away from the people who killed my father. One of their own. Flesh and blood. How could someone do that?

And to think, I'm one of them too. This is my long lost family, the family that put so much pressure on my parents to move back home when Mom was pregnant. The family that she's been hiding me from, that I thought had written us off. And here I've been staying with them for over a month with absolutely no idea of the connection.

But they must have known.

I growl under my breath and stand, brushing myself off with quick, angry swipes. I lift my hands to my eyeline, they're shaking, then I shove them to my sides and inhale a deep breath. I need to get it together.

But someone just tried to kill me! How can I possibly go back into that ballroom?

And of course, they know who I am. How could they not? And they've been trying to find my mother for me, a woman who has been hiding from these people for nearly half of her life. My memory flits back to the talisman and how I wore it around Tate at the hunting gym. He only saw a common enough crucifix since the feathers were on the back of the metal. He probably didn't think much of it considering a lot of humans wear crosses, and at least half the hunters in that gym did the same. Did he ever figure out what it was? And

Gram. Was she ashamed of me? Did she resent me for what happened? If I got the talisman back, would it make any difference for me whatsoever?

No. The truth is out there. The necklace is gone, and so is my ability to hide my true identity. The nephilim and vampires already know all about me, and I'll never be able to live a normal life again. Maybe I never was meant for normality––it's not like I'm fully human. There's no going back. Not anymore.

With a shivering breath, I stride back into the party. People aren't really dancing anymore. The humans look tired, some have already cleared out, and others look like they're in the middle of goodbyes. The nephilim, however, are energized and smiling satisfied grins. I search for the man I stole energy from so I can avoid him, but he's nowhere to be seen. So I watch the neph instead, waiting for someone to see me and act like they just pushed me off the roof.

Of course, that never happens.

Camilla is completely unruffled, and same goes for the rest of the De Luca family. None of the others seem to even notice me. Or if they do, they don't care. They're too busy buzzing off the energy they just ripped away from innocent people. I want to scream at them, to demand they do better, to confess everything that just happened to me and everything I know.

But I don't. Instead, I plaster a fake smile to my face and circulate the room, flitting from group to group to chat as if I don't have a care in the world and life is all bon-bons and roses. As if I wasn't just pushed off the roof!

Bella and Greyson saunter over with smug expressions on their faces. "My father caught your little friend. You're welcome, by the way."

I frown. What friend? "Felix? Is he okay?"

She raises an eyebrow. "Nice try."

"The bloodsucker," Greyson quips.

My mouth pops open, and my voice comes out hoarse. "Adrian?"

She grins. "That's the one. Though, I thought his name was Adrianos? Leave it to you to call him by his nickname. Mother said you're probably his lover, but none of us wanted to believe you would stoop so low."

"You don't know what you're talking about," I whisper.

She shrugs, but her eyes are glittering, and Greyson looks more awake than I've ever seen him. He also looks much healthier than he did a few hours ago. He's probably been feeding non-stop. "Well, be that as it may, my father is taking him back to the Casa and throwing him in the dungeons below the house," she continues.

"Dungeons?" I had no idea the house even had a basement.

"Of course," she speaks as if we're discussing the latest drama on a reality television show, not the fate of someone's life. "I say give him a true death."

"I'm sure you'd be happy to do the honors," Greyson chuckles darkly at his sister.

She bats her eyelashes at me. "Oh, you still don't know what my gift is yet, do you? Would you care for a demonstration?"

I couldn't care less. I'm too caught up on the whole "they caught Adrian" thing. They're going to kill him, and I may not trust him anymore, but he helped my mom and he gave me the phone. He's more on my side than these people are.

I leave the Tate children standing there, marching straight over to Camilla. She's with a group of humans and breaks away from them when she sees me coming. We meet in the middle of the dance floor, bodies swaying around us as we stare off.

"You got Adrian?" I breathe.

Her knowing eyes travel me up and down slowly, and the hairs on the back of my neck stand on end. All it would take is one touch and the woman could jump right into my memories of tonight, learning everything I know now. That would be disastrous. What was I thinking coming to her so hastily? I backpedal, dropping my voice into a grateful whisper. "What I mean is, your grandkids just told me Tate captured him. Where is he? You know he betrayed me, right?"

Her mouth flickers into a small smile. "I do know. I saw it, remember, dear?"

Of course. She saw everything that happened with him right up until Brisa died. My cheeks blush at some of those memories.

"Don't be embarrassed." She catches on immediately.

"I don't think any less of you considering what little information you had at the time. And he is rather handsome, isn't he? You wouldn't be the first to fall for a vampire's tricks."

I nod numbly.

"We have some questions for him. Important questions. Perhaps you would be persuaded to help us interrogate him?" Her eyes sparkle with dangerous fantasies, and I have to fight to keep myself from giving away my true feelings.

"Absolutely," I smile and nod, hoping I look eager and not desperate.

"Good. First thing tomorrow, then. Now, go enjoy the party. Be young. Have fun. Indulge yourself." She lifts her brows, and I know she's talking about the energy transference I never hope to experience again.

"Thank you, Camilla. For everything."

"Oh, and, Eva, one last thing."

I squeeze my hands behind my back and will myself to stay calm and my heartbeat to slow. Is this it? Is this when she grabs me and infiltrates my mind again, searching for more of Adrian? Is this when she figures out what I know? Maybe she'll throw me into the dungeon next to him.

"Merry Christmas."

So I'm some kind of freakish mutant. Memories of falling and then levitating a few feet from the ground sweep through my mind on repeat. I'm certain that's from the vamp venom, not the neph blood, and I wonder what else I can do. How much of my potential is still untapped? Maybe I should embrace this new life.

I barely sleep a wink and end up staring at the ceiling as golden morning light crawls up my bedroom walls. When I can't stand my thoughts any longer, I peel myself from the warm bed and get dressed. I'm supposed to get Felix and Seth before I go anywhere--they're staying just down the hall--but I really don't care about this family's rules anymore.

This family ... *my* family.

They're technically mine, but if they really cared about me, they wouldn't have killed my father. They took something that I'll never get back and broke my mother's heart in the process. And this whole time they've pretended that Camilla had three children, conveniently omitting the fourth. Nobody has even remarked on my appearance resembling theirs, something I'd chalked up to being part Italian. Their silence has spoken volumes--they never wanted me to find out the truth. I may have a place in the Casa, but I don't have a place with them.

I pad downstairs in search of a stairwell that could lead me down to Adrian. I think of that first day here and how my guards had seemed perturbed when I made a wrong turn on the way to the pool. I retrace my steps to find that area, then head down the quiet corridor toward what I've since learned are the staff quarters. It's not long before I find the tiny stairwell. I don't let myself think, I just act. Hurrying down the steps, my mind is set on Adrian. The temperature turns cold and the light dims, and then I'm standing in a hallway.

And I'm not alone.

"There you are," Camilla says, turning on me like she expected to see me here all along. "Good. Now we can get started."

Blood drains from my face. Did I just walk into a trap? The entire De Luca family stands behind Camilla, even the older twins, Enzo and Nicco, who are usually absent.

"You're all looking bright-eyed this morning," I smile and keep my voice chipper. "Guess you got more sleep than I did."

"I didn't sleep a wink," Chloe sighs, but there's a happiness about her that never seems to go away, even without proper sleep.

Of all the De Lucas, she and her mother, Lainey, are the only ones I kind of like. But that might be because they seem kind of clueless. I wonder how much they know about the matriarch they've let control their lives. Does Chloe know my father was the last to hold her gift? Does she even know about his existence or have they kept that from her as well? I am overflowing with questions that are far too dangerous to ask.

"Isn't this so exciting?" She slides over to me and threads her arm through mine. "Uncle Tate has been hunting this guy down for ages. Apparently he's one of the worst. And a prince! Can you believe it? We caught a prince."

"Sounds dangerous," I deadpan, and Chloe's face scrunches up as she nods.

Tate has been standing at the back of the group, but he strides forward now with his eyes pinned on me. "Yes, and we couldn't have done it without Eva."

My body goes cold, and I'm very aware that Tate knows I met with Adrian last night. Was Tate the one to push me off the roof? But why would he do that? He's worked tirelessly to keep me alive. If he wanted me dead, he's had ample opportunities to make it happen.

"Let's get this over with," Dario drawls, smirking right at me. His eyes twinkle as if he can read my mind, and I'm suddenly more suspicious of him than anyone else here. But again, I don't know what he could possibly have against me. "We all have a job to do, little girl," he says. "And if you don't do yours right, then I'll do it for you."

Bella giggles, and Bianca smirks at the back of her brother's head. "What's that supposed to mean?" I question. I still don't know what Dario's gift is. In fact, I don't know what most of them are capable of.

Dario simply chuckles as a glittering light passes over him in the blink of an eye. I stumble back with a yelp. He's no longer Dario. He's *me!* At least, he looks just like me. From my stick-straight hair to the jeans and t-shirt I threw on only a few minutes ago, it's like looking in a mirror. I've never felt more violated. That's my body. That's my face. I open my mouth to scream but no words make it out.

"Shapeshifter," he snorts, the voice that comes out sounds like Dario at least. It's jarring, but it's a chink in the armour. "I can't talk to Adrian, but I can get him to believe I'm you if the need arises."

Then all at once, he shifts back to his usual slimy self. It's no wonder I always got the ick-factor from the guy.

"And not all of our gifts can be used on vampires, so some of us will just be observing today," Camilla says, motioning for the group to follow her.

And that makes sense considering the things I've been through with Tate. I wonder about the rest of them. I know Camilla can read memories, and Chloe is the record keeper that replaced my father. Both of them have been able to impose their gifts on me. And while Tate manipulates minds, he's no longer a threat to mine. Shortly after arriving here, some of the other students told me the hulk-like twins have super tracking abilities, which doesn't affect me. Dario is a creepy shapeshifter, but what about Tate's kids, Bella and Greyson, or his wife Bianca? And what about the third De Luca son, Fredrico, and his wife Lainey? There are still so many things I don't know, things they're withholding.

The hallway is made of misshapen stones, and the floors are damp. There's no electricity down here, but someone's lit sconces along the walls. We pass by several cells with silver bars at the doors. Is Adrian the only one down here? I glance into the cells as we pass, but I don't see another soul. That doesn't mean anything. We stop at two doors next to each other. The first is a normal oak door, and the other is completely made of silver. Camilla opens the oak and ushers us inside. The sconces have been lit in here as well, and rows of arm chairs are set up facing a glass wall.

"It's a two way mirror," Lainey explains to me, patting me gently on the back. "He can't hear us, don't worry."

I blink as the others take their seats, staring through the mirror at the man on the other side. Adrian is chained to a wall with silver shackles at his arms and feet. Even in the dim light, I can see that the flesh around the shackles festers with angry red blisters. But it's the look in his eyes that haunts me. I expect him to be angry, or maybe even defeated, but he is afraid. The fear is unmistakable and raw on his usually unreadable face.

"I know you're there," he calls out, eyes trained on the glass. "I can't see you, but I can hear your heartbeats. All of them."

Bella snorts, and Camilla tells her to hush.

My stomach twists into awful barbed wire knots as I force myself to sit down and keep calm. But I'm anything but calm. Adrian isn't afraid for his own life, he's afraid for mine. And suddenly, his fear envelops me as well. Should I be afraid? What does he know about them that I haven't learned already? Mom's frantic voice comes to mind, and I wish I could be anywhere but here right now.

"Sit tight," Tate instructs the group, then he and Camilla leave the way we came and a few seconds later stride into Adrian's interrogation room.

Adrian gazes at them with a disgusted grimace. "I know what you're here to do," he snarls, "so why don't you just kill me and get it over with."

Bella clicks her tongue in disappointment. "A vampire with a death wish? Well, that's no fun."

I shoot her a dirty look, and she laughs. "Careful, Eva," she taunts, "you don't want to give yourself away. Your precious boyfriend would die for nothing."

CHAPTER 25

I ignore Bella and focus on the three people in the cell. Tate tilts his head, assessing Adrian's words. "I'm not here to kill you," he says with a sly grin. "Well, not yet anyway."

"Stop wasting my time," Adrian replies.

"Oh, did we interrupt a pressing engagement?" Tate asks. "Because as I recall, you were hanging around our party last night. You came to us, not the other way around."

Adrian glowers at Tate. "I've been hunting you for ages, don't act so surprised."

"But you weren't hunting me last night," Tate chuckles. "You were trying to get to Eva. What's your plan then? Kill her? Take her for yourself?"

Adrian says nothing, but I'll admit, I'm conflicted. I don't want them to hurt Adrian, and I don't want him to give in to them, but I'm curious about the answers as well.

"Where is the Gateway?" Camilla snaps.

"There you go. See, that wasn't so hard, was it?" Adrian laughs. "That's what you're really after. The elusive Gateway. You know we found it, and you want me to tell you where it is?"

"Of course!"

They fall silent, eager for his answer. I've never heard of this Gateway before, and have absolutely no clue what it could be. In my lessons at the Casa, nobody has mentioned that word to me. I peer around at the others, and they're all eagerly on the edge of their seats. So I guess I'm the odd one out.

"Okay, I'll tell you. . ." he pauses for dramatic effect, "nothing."

"You don't want to do that," Camilla seethes.

"Oh, believe me, I do."

"Did you forget that you're at our mercy now?"

"What mercy?" he scoffs. "You neph think you're so high and mighty, but you're no better than the monsters you hunt."

Tate steps forward. "If you're so quick to call yourself a monster, then why shouldn't we kill you after all?"

"Because I've got the answers you seek." Adrian's eyes grow dark, and his voice raspy. "You're right, Tate, I'm a monster. And when I get out of here, I am going to show you just how evil I can be. That wife of yours? Bianca? Oh, I'll start with her, but I won't stop there. Your children? Bella and Greyson? I'll hunt them down too. And when I do, I'll make sure they know their father is responsible for their deaths."

"Sick bastard," Bella mutters from beside me, growing agitated.

"Let's kill him now and get this over with," Greyson agrees. There's a rattle to his voice I've never heard before. He's afraid. And he should be.

"Trust your father and your Nana," Bianca whispers to her children. "They know what they're doing. Adrianos can't die until he gives us the information we need, but once he does, we'll take him out."

"What's the Gateway?" I ask, and they all turn on me with closed expressions.

"Have it your way," Camilla's tone is clipped as she leaves Tate there with Adrian and returns to our viewing room seconds later. She points to me. "Don't go anywhere. We'll get to you once we wear him down." And then she points to Bianca and Bella. "One of you. Bella, I think you're ready, but if you'd rather have your mother--"

"I can do it!" Bella jumps up eagerly and follows her grandmother out the door.

"You really think she's ready?" Fredrico asks his sister, and she nods reluctantly. Then everyone grows quiet as Bella and Camilla join Tate.

I don't know what I'm supposed to be seeing, but nothing happens. Bella's smug expression makes me think something is going on, but maybe it's meant for Adrian's eyes only?

"Ah, the infamous Bella De Luca-Tate," Adrian says, "Good to get a visual on you again."

"Shut your mouth," Tate snaps.

Bella turns to her father. "Daddy, it's not working."

"Vision-warps don't work on me, *Daddy*," Adrian laughs. "Don't you know I'm not your typical vampire? It'll take more than party tricks to get into my head. But maybe you ought to get your wife to come play. I hear she's quite skilled. Maybe she'll succeed where your daughter has failed."

Bella screams violently and storms from the room, and Bianca jumps up to meet her out in the hallway. I want to laugh, but I don't have a death wish. Vision-warp, huh? If I had to guess, that would be making people see things that aren't really there. My skin chills at that, and I hope that if it doesn't work on Adrian then it doesn't work on me either. I've certainly got enough vampire venom in me.

The others go next. The twins beat him up, and I have to look above them instead of directly at them as they pummel his body over and over. They punch and kick, and the more they do it, the more Adrian seems to grow stronger somehow. He's laughing hysterically by the end of it, even as blood runs down his face and mixes with his teeth. After what feels like ages, they give it up, and Lainey goes next. I don't know what she does, but the twins hold Adrian back and she touches his wounds.

I stand, face pressed to the glass as Adrian heals, his

cuts stitching themselves back together as if everything is happening in reverse.

"Oh my gosh," I whisper. Something like this is a dream come true. If I could go back and wish for any gift, this would be it.

"I know, right?" Chloe laughs.

And then Lainey steps away, and the twins begin their beating all over again. I fall back into my seat, staring at my feet. I can't watch this. Vampires can heal on their own, but what Lainey does is remarkable, and they're using it so they can beat him over and over. Again. And Again.

And again.

This continues in a cycle for hours. My stomach rolls, and I want to leave and I want to stay all at once. Deciding to take a break, I go for the door, but rough hands drag me back to my seat. I turn to glare at Fredrico. "My power will work on you, so don't make me use it," he says dryly.

"What's your power?" I raise an eyebrow.

"Sedation," Greyson says wryly. "Could've used some of that last night, Uncle. I'm exhausted. How much longer until I can go in there and finish this?"

I turn on the sour-faced boy with the chip on his shoulder. *My cousin.* "And what's your thing then, if you're so confident you can get Adrian to talk?"

He pins me with a hard stare. "How often do you have nightmares?"

The others eye Greyson with frustration. Do they

not want him to tell me?

"Never," I respond instantly, though it's a lie. I don't dream that often, but when I do they're often unsettling, and sometimes they're nightmares. Worse than nightmares. Terrors. "And anyway, that stuff isn't real. Even if I have a bad dream, I wake up and it's gone. Big deal."

"Oh, but some nightmares are real, Eva. And what I can show you has nothing to do with dreaming. Have you ever wondered what lurks in the unseen dark places? Have you ever seen something that wasn't really there, only to wonder if perhaps it was?"

I roll my eyes. "Care to be any less cryptic?"

He leans back in his seat with an exasperated sigh. "You really are dense, aren't you?"

"And I really don't understand why you hate me. What did I ever do to you? Absolutely nothing. Are you threatened or something?"

Greyson doesn't respond.

"The kid has the shadow-sight," Dario says dryly. "It means he can see the other realms. Angels. Demons. Ghosts. All that shit." He turns on his nephew with a laugh. "And he thinks he's so damn mysterious now."

I frown. "That stuff is real?"

Greyson throws up his hands. "Asks the nephilim in the middle of an interrogation with a vampire."

"Sorry," I mutter, "these things aren't widely known."

"Didn't your mother ever take you to church?" Dario asks.

"That's enough, all of you," Chloe speaks up. "I'm

trying to watch. You should too. What if he reveals something? We need to find that Gateway if we're going to ever complete our mission on Earth."

"Spoken like a true radical," Greyson rolls his eyes.

This is all so confusing to me. "What's the Gateway?"

"Can't tell you that yet," he shrugs.

"This is all a bunch of bullshit," I snap, jumping up from my seat and storming out the door and into the hallway. The others yell after me, but nobody stops me, so whatever. I'd like to see them try anyway. Never mess with an angry woman.

I push open the door to Adrian's interrogation room and stride inside. Six heads snap in my direction. Lainey's eyes are filled with relief. She's standing next to Adrian, healing him for the gazillionth time. The twins glare over all their hulking muscles. Tate raises an eyebrow, and Camilla doesn't look the least bit surprised to see me. Did they want me to interrupt like this? Well, if they did, then they just got what they wanted.

"Are you okay?" I ask Adrian.

"Leave us," he growls. "Get out of here, Eva."

"Uh, no, I don't think I'll be doing that." I've been through so much with this man, and I'm not going to let him boss me around anymore. In fact, I'm not going to let anyone.

"If you don't, they're going to kill you," I continue, hoping to surprise them all for real this time.

His eyes narrow. "You don't know what you're asking of me."

"Whatever this Gateway is, it can't be worth more than your life."

"They're going to kill me either way. And it is worth more than my life. It's worth the lives of millions."

I step back, more confused than ever. "Will someone please tell me exactly what is going on here?"

Adrian begins to speak but his words are lost the moment that Greyson strides into the room.

CHAPTER 26

ADRIAN

The boy points at Eva, and then she screams like the weight of eternity is crushing her soul. That noise splits me open, making me question everything. The Gateway has been a guarded secret for centuries that many supernaturals have sought to find. It was only recently discovered by Brisa. Not many of us even know about it, and I've never traveled there myself, though I know Mangus has been there at least twice. The neph have gone to great lengths to get to it, and Eva's pain is the only reason I'd break.

But I won't. I can't. *I can't* be responsible for the genocide that will happen if they find it.

"Torturing an innocent? You will pay for this," I say to the De Lucas and Leslie Tate. "I will not forget what you've done here."

And what they did to my prodigy before Kelli, as well as Kelli herself because it was one of their hunters who killed her. And now they're going after Eva? I'll never let them get away with it.

My voice is barely audible over the agonized screech of Eva's crying. She's babbling something about her mother being hurt, about the demons, about the darkness. They're going to break her. This is what they want. Break her so they can break me.

Camilla stalks in close, her eyes blazing. "Tell us where it is before she loses her mind. The darkness will not be kind to her."

"She's weaker than I thought," Tate adds, frowning down at her writhing form.

"They feed off of pain," the boy, Greyson, explains like it's something to be proud of. His eyes are wild with excitement as he watches, as if he's also feeding too. "And I think they also like her light. It's new for them."

They? I don't know what he has at his command, but whatever it is, it's dark. Evil. Of all the De Lucas this child is the one to fear most.

I need to think. I need to do something to stop her pain. I'm stronger than this, than them, I'm better, faster, more cunning. I've lived a thousand lifetimes, and they have but one. They can't best me. If only Camilla were inches closer, I'd be able to rip her throat out with my teeth. It would be so quick, so brutal, that even their healer wouldn't be able to do a thing to stop her death. I eye her aged skin, reminded of tissue paper. It would be so easy . . . And then the others would lose their tempers and kill me. Or kill Eva. Maybe both. But they wouldn't have the information they wanted, and their matriarch would be gone.

"You kill her, and you do my kind a favor," I spit. "We know what she is. She killed our queen."

But they don't know what Sebestian wants to do with her. If they did, then surely they'd cut her down immediately.

"I think you do care." Tate strides forward. "I think you care very, very much. If you didn't, you'd have given up the location already."

"How do you figure that?"

Eva crawls to her hands and knees now, heaving. Her body is in a fight or flight response. She started in fight mode, but is now caving in on herself, as if trying to chase away shadows. I will her to be strong, to use what she has to defend herself. She has light in her somewhere. Light that might kill me, but if she were to unleash it, it might destroy those shadows. It might stop this. Save her.

But her hands don't glow. And her body stays rigid. And her cries only get louder.

"You care because you love her," Tate laughs. "You care because you know what we're going to do once we find the Gateway. And mind you, we will find it. For a vampire, it's pretty funny that you're acting like you don't want blood on your hands. Such a hypocrite. You'll always have blood on your hands. And soon you'll rot hell with blood on your hands."

"And so will you."

He rolls his eyes. "You can help us or you can die, but either way we're going to find the Gateway. Might as well save Eva first."

I look him square in the eye. "Fine. I choose death."

He steps back and kicks Eva lightly. She doesn't seem to process it, or even that any of us are here talking about her. "So you'd choose her death?"

"You can't put that on me." I press my arms up where the chains snag against my flesh, burning me further. I don't care--I press harder, trying to break free. It's useless. "I'm not the one hurting her, you are!"

"So you do love her," Tate roars. "And you're going to let us drive her mad? Kill her right in front of you? You're more vile than I thought."

My fangs extend, and I cackle. "You aren't going to kill your greatest weapon. This is a bluff. A sick and twisted game that I'm not playing."

I close my mouth and look away, concentrating on the cracks in the walls and shutting my mind away. I've had great practice in putting my emotions aside, and this will be no different.

Someone else enters the room then, and whatever Greyson is doing stops because Eva's cries peter out and turn to muffled sobs. I blink at Fredrico, one of the other De Luca sons, and one of the few whose gift I wasn't able to learn during my years of keeping tabs on the family. Brisa made sure all the nephilim factions were under constant surveillance and had given the De Lucas to me after my unfortunate run-in with Tate years ago. I'm still not sure if she did that to punish me for failing my prodigy or as a way to stoke my desire for revenge.

"One touch from me, and you'll be sedated," Fredrico says, strolling up to me and giving away his play. "And do you know what happens next?"

"You're not supposed to tell me what you're going to do before you do it," I mock. "Where's the fun in that?"

I've never met a sedator before, but they're dangerous. My fangs pang in protest.

"I'll sedate you, and then I'll extract your venom." His eyes are cold. "Venom isn't always easy to come by, and yours must be quite strong. We could use it in our war efforts, don't you think?"

So they know about the venom. I'd suspected it, but couldn't get confirmation. Well, here it is, and it makes me sick.

"Touch me and die," I glare at the lanky man. "Go ahead. See if it works. Most of you can't affect me. Not even ghost-boy over here can hurt me."

I don't actually know if Greyson sees ghosts, but it's a close enough guess. The kid glares, and I swear Eva holds in a laugh. She must be feeling much better. Nobody moves.

"Well, are you going to do it or not? I haven't got all day. The sun will be setting soon. Better get moving if you think you're going to extract my venom and then throw me out for the sun to burn."

"We could always stake you," Fredrico quips.

"But you won't. Where's the fanfare in that when you can watch your enemy go up in flames? Ah, don't feel bad, I'd do the same thing to you in a heartbeat."

"You don't have a heartbeat."

"Good point."

Fredrico's ego gets the best of him, just as I'd hoped. He reaches out to touch me, and I'm wagering on one thing: that his power won't be stronger than I am. Because I'm fast, I'm old, and I've been through enough close-encounters over the centuries to know how to survive.

My wager pays off. His touch sends a wave of drowsiness through me, but not enough to put me to sleep. I'm all out of patience. All out of good ideas. All out of mercy.

There's nothing left. Not for these people.

Still manacled, I snatch Fredrico's wrist in my hand and tug him to me, making good on my promise. It's so quick. The flesh of his throat is warm and soft under my razor fangs. I slice him right open, his blood splattering across the room, and drink him in before biting deeper, ripping his throat out.

So much glorious blood.

It pours down me, and then I'm dropping his body at my feet, rivers of red slipping down my chin. "Who's next?"

More screaming––more for me to feed on.

Now they'll stake me. It's over. But they'll have to be brave enough to get near me first.

"You!" I growl at Greyson. "You're next. Come join your uncle."

Tate pushes his son out the door while the healer screams, grabbing onto Fredrico's body and hollering about her husband. Even now, she's trying to heal him. It won't work. And if she gets any closer, I'll kill her too. I'll kill every last one of them if given the chance.

Camilla is saying something to me in Italian that I hardly care to listen to. Something along the lines of comply or die, but I drown it out.

I expect to deal with a stake at any moment, but I don't get one. They all leave, dragging the body out with them, a smear of crimson marking the floor. Tate picks Eva up and carries her away. Just as they're closing the door, I catch her eyes. They hold onto my gaze, possessive and strong. She's no longer crying.

Is she on their side or mine?

Night must come because hours inch by, but there's no way for me to know for sure. They keep me locked up. Isolated. Waiting.

At least I fed. I feel amazing, and I don't regret what I did. Maybe I should. But I never pretended to be anything other than what I am. I've killed before, and I'll kill again. They're the fools for thinking they could expect anything else from me.

Anything less.

Hours pass. Days? Minutes? I don't know anymore, until the door swings open again. Four pairs of legs walk toward me. I gaze up, assuming the De Lucas are back, but it's Evangeline standing before me with a grim expression on her pretty face. At her sides are her two hunter friends, Felix and Seth. I'm surprised to see them. But not as surprised as I am to see the fourth person.

"Mangus," I breathe. "You came."

Eva must have used the "In Case of Emergency" number that I'd programmed into the phone. Does that mean she trusts me again? Will she leave with me? I don't know what I'll do if she breaks me out of here but refuses to come along.

"At your service, brother." Mangus nods. "Now let's go. We've got things to do. People to see."

He's got nothing to do or see, but leave it to Mangus to keep things light. Eva gets to work on my chains, producing a key to attack the locks. I have no idea how she managed to get a key, and I want to kiss her in gratitude. Felix and Seth stand in the corner, apprehension evident on their faces, but here nonetheless. I guess I'll let the fact that they're vampire hunters slide for the moment considering they're here to save my ass.

"And where are we going then?" I ask Mangus just as Eva manages to get me unshackled. The relief is palpable.

"Don't you know?" Mangus laughs. "There's this Gateway that everyone is fighting over. Guess we'd better get there and make sure the wards are still strong. You're in luck because I know just where to go."

CHAPTER 27

"How did you manage to get to me?" Adrian asks, bewildered. His hair is a bloodied halo around his face, rings of exhaustion circling shallow eyes. But at least he's still alive. The Gateway must be important. I thought for sure they would have staked him after he killed Fredrico.

I'm still angry with Adrian, but I'm also proud of myself for coming this far. The fact that I'm here is nothing short of a miracle. "It was the hardest thing I've ever had to pull off. Now hurry up, let's go, and I'll explain on the way."

We sneak back out into the hallway, and I handle any silver in our path, grateful that only bothered me during the three nights of transition. Adrian is weak so Mangus holds him up under an arm as they shuffle along. "I've never heard vampires make so much noise," I hiss, and they stop.

"Is she always this pleasant?" Mangus asks Adrian.

"Only in the mornings," Adrian replies dryly, and my cheeks burn. Felix and Seth exchange a disgusted look that makes me want to slap them both, but there's no time for that. And I shouldn't be so smug because we could be caught at any moment.

"Follow me," I whisper-yell.

The house has silver bars on the windows and doors, but Mangus got in, so I'm determined to get out. The best route won't be through any of those doors or windows, and that's because it won't be what the De Luca family will expect. I quickly lead them out of the dungeon and up to the center atrium on the main floor, passing the guards the four of us gagged and bound on the way.

Just as we sweep into the muggy room with the overgrown plants, unseen alarms blare, and my heart drops.

"You can levitate, right?" I ask Mangus, and he snorts.

"What do you take me for?" he says, "Of course, I can levitate."

"Well, Hugo couldn't, so it's not an unreasonable question."

Mangus turns on Adrian. "What does she know of Hugo?"

My cheeks warm. "Later. What about you, Adrian? Do you have enough strength?"

"Yes, and I'll carry you." He's mighty confident for

having just been tortured, beaten, and held captive for the last forty-eight hours.

"Adrian, you carry Seth. Mangus, you carry Felix. And I'll worry about myself."

All four men stare at me, and before I can address their obvious lack of faith in me, I'm floating in midair.

Mangus whistles low. "Impressive. How much venom did you get?"

"Enough to do that," Adrian says.

Felix and Seth's jaws drop, and Mangus mutters something about having seen it all now. Then he throws Felix over his shoulder, and I almost laugh at my large Cuban-American friend's protests.

"They're in here!" a man yells, and footsteps sound from the hallway outside the atrium.

"We've got to move!" I hiss. "They've got silver bullets!"

Adrian scoops Seth up, and then we're all flying for the ceiling. I curl in on myself, my back a battering ram as I fly through the glass. I hit it hard, shattering the pane around me, shards raining down. I press on, concentrating. I'd practiced in a room a bunch over the last few days but figured that all it really took was concentration, otherwise it was easy. But that was a few feet off the ground, and this is entirely different. We continue up into the sweeping blackness, and my gut clenches. I try not to think about falling, so instead, I focus on the cool, still night to distract me. The moon hangs bright and full in the sky, and with the added benefit of the venom, the world is illuminated to near daylight.

We zip up and away from the Casa, and I allow myself to relax. And then giggle, thrilled that levitating has come so easily. Just as that thought hits me, I plummet and yelp, the ground coming at me fast. Someone swoops ahead of me, catching me in his other arm. Mangus.

I cry out with relief. "Don't get cocky," he says, "that's how people get killed."

"Thank you for catching me," I say through ragged breaths. "I always thought you didn't like me."

"I didn't," Mangus responds, "but I like Adrian, and he likes you."

"Can we not have this conversation right now?" Felix groans from Mangus's other arm. His eyes are round saucers taking in the blur of landscape as Mangus flies us over the city and out toward the sea. "I think I'm going to be sick."

"Get sick, and I'll drop you," Mangus warns.

"You wouldn't," I snap. To Felix I add, "He wouldn't."

Mangus only growls, indicating that he, in fact, would. It doesn't matter though, because Felix doesn't get sick, and soon we're flying over lapping ocean waves and toward a small island off the coast. Adrian isn't far behind us, and even over the rushing wind, I can hear Seth saying something about not being a good swimmer.

We land on the island, which is nothing more than a

big rock with an old lighthouse and a dock with a couple of boats tied up.

"Our ride will be here soon," Mangus says. "Hang tight everybody."

"How did you do it?" Adrian turns on us. "You saved me."

"You could've gotten out," Mangus argues. "You always do. How many times have you been in situations like this before?"

Adrian shakes his head. "This time was different. I lost my temper, I killed one of the higher-ups. They would've kept trying their powers on me until I grew weak enough for them to actually work. They wouldn't have let me live much longer."

So supernaturals aren't entirely immune to angelic gifts, which explains a lot of what I saw two days ago during the interrogation. I tuck that information away for later.

I think he's right about them killing him, but I don't say it. The De Luca family has been a mess since Fredrico died, and their anger has been as thick as smoke. "I faked Greyson's little torture bit," I explain. "It worked at first, but I was quick to fight it off. I already knew that was his thing, so I pretended the shadows were still after me, and everyone bought it."

Adrian nods, leveling me with a stare that makes my insides twist. "You're a good actress, Angel."

Angel . . . I'm not sure I like that nickname anymore. I shrug. "When I need to be."

Once Adrian had killed Fredrico, the entire Casa fell to pieces. People were crying, whispering in corridors, there was even some wailing behind closed doors from a few of the family members. All those emotions hitting the house at once made it easy for me to do what I needed to get Adrian out of there. It was the perfect distraction.

"They expected me to be out of it as I recovered from his attack on me. So I walked around like a zombie, and nobody talked to me for a while. The first thing I did was lift a phone off a staff member and called that 'In Case of Emergency' number you left for me."

"You lost the phone I gave you?" Adrian raises an eyebrow.

"You gave her a phone?" Seth interrupts. "When did that happen?"

I snap my fingers. "None of that matters anymore. Listen. I called it, and your pal Mangus here answered. When I told him you were in trouble, he immediately offered to rescue you, and we worked out a plan."

Truth be told, I was floored when Mangus answered and so quickly offered his help. The guy never liked me, but this wasn't about me, it was about Adrian, which showed me how much he cared for him. It gave me hope and a reason to do the risky thing I did next. "Getting the keys off Camilla had been a lot harder."

"Yeah, that woman doesn't seem like the type you could pull one over on," Felix admits.

"And she's scary as hell," I let out a laugh.

"She's not so bad," Seth argues. "Remember what Tate said? She can be trusted." He turns and gazes out at the water. "Maybe we should go back. They're not that bad."

The vampires scrunch up their faces, and I quickly explain how my friends have been continually manipulated by Tate's mind tricks. Not that either of these guys have room to talk, considering vampires compel humans. It's almost the same thing.

"Go on about the keys," Mangus interrupts, gazing at me with new eyes. "I want to hear this part. You're more interesting than I gave you credit for, Angel."

"Don't call her that," Adrian hisses, "Only I can call her that."

"The only person who has permission to call me that is my mother." I roll my eyes and go on. "Anyway, I went to visit her in her study to offer my condolences. She'd been an emotional wreck, not like herself at all, and I hate to say it, but I took advantage of that and snagged the ring of keys when she wasn't looking."

I pull them from my pocket now and toss them out to sea, my superhuman strength sending them whizzing ridiculously far. I still feel a little bad about taking advantage of Camilla, but I'd realized that these people weren't on my side the moment they'd taken me to that party to feed on human auras. Everything had gotten so complicated since walking into the casino that day back in August. I'd always seen the world in black and white, and both the vampires and the nephilim had me questioning that, making me feel like everyone was a solid mix of gray.

I don't want to be gray.

There have to be good guys out there, and I'm going to be one of them. I have a choice of doing right or wrong, and I'm going to do what's right, and if I end up making a wrong choice, then I'm going to correct it. Staying with the De Luca family would've turned me into someone I'm not. I think of my dad. How hard it must have been for him to get away from them. That choice ended up costing him his life. I'm following in his footsteps, and just have to hope I get a better ending to my story.

Felix breaks the silence next. "I'm pretty sure that's when Eva came and got us," he says to the vampires, "she asked us to come with her, and since we swore to Tate that we wouldn't leave her and that we'd protect her no matter what, we had no choice but to agree to her terms."

Mangus's nostrils flare, and his pupils dilate. "You're hunters, though? And you've made promises to Tate?"

My friends nod slowly and it's like an invisible goes up between them and the vampires.

"You're lucky you're not dead," Mangus says. "That I didn't kill you the second I saw you."

True to his word, the viking vampire prince had shown up at my door an hour ago. He'd broken into the house, claiming that he was stronger than most vampires and therefore had no trouble getting into homes, even if they were inhabited by neph. I hadn't questioned him––the older the vamp, the more powerful and skilled they can be. I don't know when vikings were around, but Mangus is as old as them.

My friends are clearly uncomfortable and inching away from the vampires. They don't have stakes or guns on them. They've got no defense, and the sun is still hours from rising. At any moment the vampires could kill them for being hunters.

"They can be trusted," I say to Mangus, trying to comfort my friends, although a thread of fear weaves down my spine. "The fact that they're here and didn't cause any issues getting Adrian out is proof enough."

Mangus doesn't seem convinced. "One mistake, and I'll kill them."

I gape at him, then at Adrian. He shrugs. "You're my priority, Eva. If they attempt to double-cross us, then I'll kill them if Mangus doesn't beat me to it."

And I know he will. These men mean every word, which is exactly why my friends *must* go home.

CHAPTER 28

"Do you guys have your passports, money, things like that?" I turn on Seth and Felix. When they nod, I muster up the courage I need to do the right thing, even though it's going to hurt the relationships I've spent weeks rebuilding. "Then you should go." I point to the boats bobbing at the docks. "Take one of those and get out of here. Go back home and return to your lives."

"We're not leaving you," Seth replies first, surprising me.

"Yeah, Eva, whatever this is, we're in it." Felix nods, eyes earnest.

"Eva is right," Mangus says, "it's not safe for you."

"It's not safe for any one of us," Felix argues, jabbing his fingers at the vampires. "You just don't want hunters around, but guess what? I don't trust you with Eva any more than you trust me with her."

"We could make you go," Mangus snarls. His temper flares, and it might be the first time I've seen him like this. He's usually so cold and aloof. He's different than he used to be, but that was when his wife was still alive. I know she died being blamed for his death, which is part of why I was so stunned when he'd been the one on the other end of that "In Case of Emergency" phone number.

Seth stands taller. "We're not old enough to be compelled. So what are you going to do about it?"

The tension between our little ragtag group is as dangerous as a taut wire about to snap, and whoever pulls on it next will likely end up getting hit. "That's enough." I hold up my hands in surrender and turn on my friends. "I appreciate everything you've done for me. I love you guys, but the people who are after me could hurt you, and you're not going to be able to fight them off."

Because now I'll have vampires *and* nephilim on my tail.

"When are you going to get it?" Felix rakes a hand through his dark curls and levels me with an exasperated look. "We're here by choice. Sure, we made a promise to Tate but that was only because we care about you. Protecting you is what we wanted, too. Don't treat us like a liability."

But that's exactly what they are.

"I'm sorry," my voice cracks, and their faces fall, but I can't give up on them. Not yet. "I've tried to tell you multiple times, but every time I do, you just gloss over it like it's nothing. The truth is that Tate is the reason you care so much about my safety. He used his mind manipulation to get you to trade in your normal lives to be here for me. I mean, just think about what you've been saying tonight. Don't you see that I'm right?"

It seems so obvious. He even said himself that Tate made them promise.

Felix shakes his head and steps forward. "You're wrong, Eva. You're my sister's best friend and have been a part of my family for years. It wouldn't matter what Tate did or didn't do, I'd still be here."

Is that true, though? Because while he always treated me well, it was never like this. Our relationship has been a rollercoaster since August, and I need to get him out, for his own sake more than anything. "I'm no good for you," I say, reaching out and squeezing his hand. He squeezes back. "You had such a bright future until all this happened. Think of your family. They're probably worried sick about you. And think of Ayla." Last I saw her, she'd gone into an agoraphobic depression and locked herself in her room and everyone out of her life. "She needs you now more than ever. She's your family, not me."

The unmistakable humming pulse of helicopter blades slices through the night, weak at first and growing stronger. Buzzy adrenaline shoots through me. "That will be the De Luca family," I hiss. "They have a helicopter. We need to take cover."

"You think the De Lucas are the only ones with deep pockets?" Mangus chuckles darkly. "That's our ride, honey. Right on time."

"And we're going with you," Felix adds. "That's final."

Mangus and Adrian catch each other's eyes, and I wonder what they're thinking.

The noise grows, and a couple of minutes later the wind wraps around us as the helicopter lands. The five of us run to it, and Adrian lifts me up to get in first. I turn back to a blur of movement so fast I almost miss it. But apparently my friends don't see it in time because a second later Mangus and Adrain are dropping them off at the distant docks. A second later, the vampires are back, climbing in next to me, and we're lifting into the air while my friends are sprinting toward us up the pier. But they're not fast enough--nobody is as fast as the vampires, and the chopper is quick.

"I'm sorry," I yell out the door, hoping my voice isn't lost to the noise. "Be safe!"

They're hollering something back, but I can't hear them, and then Mangus is sliding the door shut and falling back into the seat beside me. The chopper veers to the right, and we're zipping off over the sea. I've yet to decide if we're running to or from the greater danger, but at least I'm leaving the Casa.

"We've got a private jet waiting for us in Geneva. Then it's a three hour flight to where we're going," Mangus says. "We'll get there before sunrise. Get some rest."

"I don't need any rest. I'm fine."

Mangus clicks his tongue but doesn't say anything more. The viking is sitting next to me, and across from us, Adrian is slumped over the seat. His normally vibrant blue eyes are pale, there's blood turning his hair copper, and his cheeks are sunken in. "You need to feed." I eye him with a frown.

"I'm fine," he mumbles.

Mangus leans over Adrian to say something to the human in the cockpit, and we start to descend.

"What are you doing?" Adrian asks at the same time I say, "Where are we going?"

"Adrian needs to eat sooner rather than later, so we're making a quick pit stop in Rome," Mangus replies gruffly.

"No!" Adrian roars, forcing his body up and glaring at Mangus. "The priority is getting Eva out of here. Rome will slow us down, plus it's not our territory. I can eat later."

I must admit, I also really want to get out of Italy.

"The priority is getting all of us safely to the Gateway." Mangus levels Adrian with a hard stare. "We do what I say, and then we'll do what you say, brother."

"What's the Gateway?" I demand, then sigh. "Actually, hold that thought, first, Adrian does need to eat." I can't believe I'm doing this, but seeing him this exhausted has me panicked. I'm still angry with him, but I don't like this weak side of him, not when I can do something about it. I extend my wrist. "Drink."

Both men flash me strange looks.

"Absolutely not," Adrian hisses. "It's forbidden anyway."

"Says who?" I press. "I don't see Brisa around to enforce anything, do you? You need blood, and I need to get out of Italy as quickly as possible, so it's a win-win."

Mangus gives me a hard look. "And how do we know you're not becoming addicted to the venom?"

Maybe I am, but this truly isn't about that. "Look, do you want to get out of here faster or do you want to stop and waste time?"

They both stare at my wrist, and then Mangus nods to Adrian before leaning over to instruct the pilot to get back on course. Adrian grabs my wrist and yanks me into his lap. I expect him to bite the delicate flesh there, but he doesn't.

"Make me stop," Adrian says to his brother. "Don't you dare let me kill her."

"I wouldn't dream of it," Mangus winks.

Before I can process how their conversation makes me feel, Adrian is shifting in closer, his body pressing to mine. He runs his nose along my cheek and down my jaw, inhaling my scent. "I can't say no to you," he whispers. "Do you understand what that means, Angel?"

"I hardly doubt that's true." One thing I know about Adrian is he'll do anything to get his way. Even if it means waiting a century, he'll wait . . . and then he'll strike. His mouth inches toward mine, that intoxicating scent wafting over me, and my insides flip. Memories of being with him and then being left by him pummel me, and I shift back. I can't kiss those lips again. I'll be lost if I do.

So I lift my wrist to him again. "Take what you need." There's a long pause, and then he's moving my wrist out of the way and going for my neck. I arch into him, letting him, the anticipation blushing through me. The bite stings at first, like the cut of a razor, but the venom slides into my veins, and I'm soon flooded with bliss. A vulnerability I haven't felt with him since we slept together blossoms within, closeness and openness all at once. I want to cry, to scream, to laugh, to do everything and nothing all at once. I'm so overcome with emotion that it's peacefully paralyzing, and my entire body relaxes into his grip.

With Hugo and Brisa this experience had been horrifying, but with Adrian it's wonderful, and I suddenly know what Mangus said about it being possible to get addicted to this. How could I not? I could go on and on like this forever. I moan and lean into him, his fangs pushing in deeper. And then he's rearing back with a hiss, and I feel lost. Our eyes meet over shared gasps. His are rimmed in red and hungry with desire.

"Have you had enough?" I rasp out, inching back.

His entire demeanor changes from feral animal to chastised puppy, and his eyes drop, fangs retreating. "Yes, thank you." He carefully lifts me from his lap, putting me back in the seat next to Mangus who's watching us with an equal mix of interest and heartbreak. I've always had a hard time getting a read on Mangus, but now his emotions are plain on his face. He misses his wife. He's angry, hurt, and most of all, heartbroken.

The moment is too much, and we turn away to stare out the windows. There's nothing to see but dark sky, clouds, and night. *So much night.* They're used to living this way, but I'm not. I can't ever become like them, it would ruin me.

"Alright, guys," I gather up my courage and start the conversation that needs to be had. "It's time to answer some of my questions."

Adrian's lips thin, and Mangus bristles, but I don't back down.

CHAPTER 29

ADRIAN

What will happen if Mangus realizes the truth about Eva? If he figures out just how much power she's acquired, he may kill her or side with Sebastian's way of thinking. So even though my vampire brother has more answers than I currently do, I take the lead. I gaze at Eva, unable to take my eyes off her. Her blood has given me a new sense of purpose. I've never tasted anyone so sweet––and with so much potential. I can't let anyone else have her. I have to keep her safe, and that means telling her as much truth as I can in front of Mangus.

"I've wanted to be honest with you for a long time, Angel," I say, careful to keep my voice steady. "I hope you know that."

She raises a skeptical eyebrow, and it's the most Eva-like thing she's done all night that I have to fight back a grin. There's my girl. "What I know is your words and your actions don't always line up, so you'll excuse me if I'm a little apprehensive."

"That's fair, but I could only say and do so much without my maker stopping me." Surely she understands that about vampires by now.

"You're saying Brisa is to blame for your shortcomings?" she snorts.

I sit up, my patience beginning to wear thin, but I'm also desperate. I can't lose her again. "That's exactly what I'm saying. So many times back at that palace I wanted to tell you exactly what was going on, but my maker refused me. I've done the best I could to keep you safe. But I see now how badly I failed you, and I'll never forgive myself."

"Since when are you so dramatic?" Mangus scoffs, interrupting me. His eyes are rimmed with disdain, and I worry where this conversation could be headed. "Come on, enough with this pathetic lovers' quarrel." He turns on Eva. "You can forgive Adrian later or not, but enough about that. You want to know about the Gateway, correct? Let's talk about the important matters."

I'd argue that our "lovers' quarrel" is the important matter.

She breaks our gaze to glare at Mangus. "Yes, but I'd also love to know why Brisa believed you died. Or are you going to blame everything on your maker as well?" She shoots me a quick roll of her eyes. "Being unaccountable for your actions is so unattractive."

Ouch. I can't help but laugh, and Mangus does the

same. "I didn't realize you were so feisty," he says to her, and then to me, "I can see why you like her."

"Enough," she waves her hands, her cheeks going slightly pink. "Just tell me about your supposed death, and then let's talk about the Gateway."

"Very well," Mangus sighs and leans back in his chair. I'll admit I'm interested as well. I've only heard bits and pieces, but I'd like to know the whole story. "It actually starts with the Gateway, so I can tell you both in one story. Have you heard of the Gateway before, Eva?"

She shakes her head. "The only Gateway I know is a run-down shopping mall."

Mangus snorts. "No, not a shopping mall. The Gateway is a hidden portal to the fae realm," he explains. "The fae have kept its location a well-hidden secret until Brisa's agents recently tracked it down. I lead the team that found it."

Eva is statue-still. I'm not sure if she believes him or not, but he's not lying. Fae are real, but since they stopped coming to the human realm long ago, they haven't been on our radar.

"You're confirming that faeries are real?" she questions, but there's something in her eyes that's not completely honest. Maybe she already knew about them. Considering where she's been lately, I wouldn't be surprised if she already hates them.

"How much did the nephilim teach you?" He shakes his head. "Yes, of course, they're real. Fae is the term we use for magical creatures that are connected to Earth's elements. Faeries, trolls, elves, mermaids, leprechauns, boggarts, dryads, and so on and so forth. You know what I'm talking about, right?"

She lets out a strangled laugh. "I guess so."

"There are three Earthly realms––the human realm where we're all living, the fae realm where they live, and then the spirit realm, but we don't know much about that."

I think of Greyson and wonder what he could tell us about spirits.

"Many of the fae used to travel between human and fae realms, but when vampires, nephilim, and were-wolves grew in number, they retreated to their realm and stayed there. The Gateway is the only known portal between those realms that hasn't already been destroyed."

"So why did Brisa want to find it?" she asks.

"There are rumors of fae witches who will grant wishes to those who find them," I pipe up. "Is that what happened to you, Mangus?"

He gives me a slow grimace, probably because I'm going to make him reveal more than he'd intended. "Well, it turns out fae witches don't grant wishes, but they do make bargains."

I swallow. Of course, it's not that easy. Nothing ever is.

"So that's why you're alive when Brisa said you were dead?" Eva breathes out slowly, her mind at work.

I don't know how much more he'll divulge, but he

gives in to her easily, which only causes my suspicions about her abilities to grow. This isn't good.

I keep a close eye on Mangus.

Does he realize what's happening? Will he kill her if he figures it out?

"I made a deal to break the blood bond with Brisa," he confesses. "It was all set to go through on the final day of October. She would assume me dead, and Katerina and I would be free to live out eternity without her ruling over us anymore."

If I'd known a fae witch could do such a thing, I'd have gone looking for one long ago, and I haven't been treated nearly as poorly as Mangus has. When he got engaged to Katerina, Brisa was threatened and angry. She'd allowed them to be together but had made their lives hell, stripping them of a coven and not allowing them to make any prodigy.

They'd spent decades on the move, slaves to Brisa's errands, enforcing her rule of law whether they liked it or not. It's no wonder he found a way out of that, but I can see the torture in his eyes now. It's worse than the days of Brisa because at least before he still had his wife. Now he faces an eternity without her, and little to show for it.

"What was the bargain? What did you give up?" Eva asks, and his face crumples.

"I think that's enough," I interrupt. Mangus doesn't normally answer questions like this, and I can't have him figuring out what's going on here––just how much power Eva has over us. I first realized it when she insisted her friends not come along with us back on that island. I'd been overcome with the need to make her wishes a reality.

But Mangus ignores me. Further proof. "I owe her a favor," he says. "Any favor that she can call upon at any time. Considering the fae never travel to our realm, I figure it won't be a problem."

Oh, brother, you're smarter than this.

Eva's face softens, and she pats his shoulder. Mangus has always been so hard to read, his emotions a glacier with very little on the surface, but right now he's entirely on display. He doesn't even flinch when Eva touches him, which wouldn't have happened with the old Mangus. The old Mangus was like the rest of the princes––stoic, professional, lethal, and no-nonsense.

Timing is a cruel mistress sometimes. If he hadn't made that bargain, Katerina would still be here. And Eva would've still killed Brisa, so he'd have been free of the blood bond either way. But things rarely work out the way they should, a lesson I've had to learn repeatedly since my human death. It's better to plan for the worst, especially if you want to stay alive.

"So why are we going to the Gateway?" Eva asks.

I think I already know. Mangus has figured things out. He wants to make another bargain.

"Sebastian wants to take the throne," Mangus says. It's no surprise that Seb is a greedy bastard, but I was expecting him to do something else. "We're going to make sure that doesn't happen." He turns to me. "It's time to tell her about the council."

My energy stores were so weak when they broke me out of the De Luca's place that I wasn't paying too much attention to where we were heading or why. But now we're in the air, and Eva is here, and all I want is to get her to safety. I'm not sure why she needs to know about the council, it might put her in danger to know too much.

"Go on," he prompts. "She's along for the ride now, might as well tell her what she's getting herself into."

But even I'm not sure what that is.

I narrow my eyes, but do as I'm asked and explain. Eva nods along, and when I'm finished, she doesn't say anything for a long time.

"On the one hand, I think the world would be better off without vampires, but I'm not as radical as I used to be, and I'm not like the other nephilim." Eva very well could be bluffing. She's hated vampires from the moment I met her, but I don't doubt her out loud. I can't risk what Mangus will do. "But on the other hand, that sounds like a better idea than a crazy monarch who has all the control. Brisa was awful, and Sebastian would be too."

"It's done. There will be no monarchy. The elections are almost finished, and then our council will be meeting soon."

"Do you really think voting is going to be enough?" Mangus deadpans. "How long have you been alive? How many monarchies and governments have we seen fall in our time on Earth?"

"Voting is all we have."

"Well, we need more than that, we need another blood bond, not a royal one, a council one, and that's why we're going to the Gateway."

My mouth pops open. It's brilliant. But it's also terribly dangerous. "You'd be willing to risk the future of our kind on the mercy of fae?"

"If we don't, there will be constant strife among the vampires, and Sebastian will never give up." Then he turns to Eva and drops the bomb. "He wants you, and he's got thousands of vampires looking for you. A council is in your benefit as much as ours."

Her face has gone ashen, and she doesn't move for several long seconds before nodding. "So what am I supposed to do? I'll do anything to get back to a normal life."

Mangus laughs bitterly. "Wouldn't we all. That's not how it works for people like us. Not anymore. Might I make a suggestion? Make your own bargain with the fae witch while you've got the chance."

"No," I snap. "She will do no such thing."

Eva slinks down in her seat and glares at me. "Do you have any better ideas?"

Not really, and she's stubborn as hell. If she's got an idea in her head, then she's going to act on it. So much for her just being along for the ride.

CHAPTER 30

"Welcome to Ireland," Mangus says when our jet lands an hour before sunrise. Rolling hills stretch in every direction around us, and I wish I could see the colors a bit better at night. We're being dropped off in the middle of nowhere, the adrenaline is gone, and I'm so exhausted that it's hard to muster up any excitement. We're in a country I've always wanted to visit, but once again, I'm no tourist.

Luckily the switch over from helicopter to private jet in Geneva was uneventful. And on our way off of the airplane, Mangus compelled the human pilots to forget all about us.

"There are not a lot of safe houses for vampires in Ireland," Adrian remarks as we watch the jet turn and taxi up the runway. It's a tiny airport and I'm sure those pilots will be out of here as soon as they gas up.

I spin in a slow circle, frowning at the structure-less

land, and worry Adrian might be on to something. There's only the tiny airport but it's got lights on and humans inside. They need somewhere safe and private to hide from the sun that won't be tracked by hunters, but I have faith in their instincts to find just the place.

"Let's go," Mangus rises into the air, and Adrian lifts me into his arms.

"You're tired," he whispers against my ear as we take flight. "You rest, and I'll fly."

Maybe he's right, but I should probably fly myself since I'm still grappling with the idea of forgiving him. I'm still mad. I'm still hurt. But the truth is, bearing witness to that beating changed my perspective on our situation. I've realized how much he matters to me. I shouldn't want him anymore, but I do. I shouldn't forgive him, but I feel myself already starting to. And I've missed him. I've missed him so badly that it carved out my stomach and slowed my heart and fuzzied my head.

A few minutes later, we land on the grassy lawn of an old stone building with a few crumbling outbuildings. There's nothing else here.

"What is this place?" Adrian asks. "An abandoned farm?"

From the overgrown garden of dead brambles, the falling-down fences, and the fields beyond, I'd guess the same thing. "If nobody owns it, you won't have to get permission to enter."

Adrian scoffs. "Permission to enter is one of our

flimsiest weaknesses anyway. I'm not worried about that." He sighs and heads toward the front door.

"Your boyfriend is a bit of an elitist." Mangus winks at me. "Poor guy is used to penthouse suites and palaces."

My heart skips at the word *boyfriend,* and I'm suddenly not sure what to do with my hands.

Adrian laughs, motioning to the decrepit house. "And you're telling me that with our global network and endless resources, this is the best you could do?"

"Beggars can't be choosers."

Their teasing allows me to relax.

"The vampire network is vast," Mangus explains. "We hacked into Brisa's accounts after her passing and were able to access them in their entirety: every coven, every property, every ally, all of it. But if I could hack that information, then it's possible others could as well, so it's best if we stay off the grid the closer we get to the Gateway. It's location is one she didn't record anywhere, and it's best that others don't find it."

Adrian pulls open the door and the entire thing comes off its hinges. He tosses it to the grass. "I hope you know what you're doing."

Mangus grins. "Worst case scenario, we dig like the old days."

I wonder about how many worst-case scenarios these men have been in, guessing that their stories would be more entertaining than anything I could dream up.

"You're talking to someone who was recently captured by the De Lucas, so you'll excuse me if I don't feel confident right now."

Mangus points to me. "Because she's your weak spot, and they knew it."

The guilt follows me into the old house with all its dust bunnies, peeling paint, and graffitied walls. I bet it has seen its fair share of squatters and bored teenagers looking for a place to party. But is it empty? I listen quietly, focusing on my heightened hearing, and don't find a beating heart or slow exhale other than my own. Unless a vampire is lying in wait, nobody is here.

We find an old staircase and head to the basement. There's not much down here. The floors are dirt, the ceiling is low, and there's no furniture. It's nothing like the opulence these vampires have grown accustomed to. But there are three rooms at the back of the basement without any windows, which is all the vamps need to hide.

"This is the exact opposite of what I had in mind," Adrian says ruefully to Mangus, who laughs. "But thank you for saving my life."

Mangus claps him on the back. "You would've done the same for me." Then he wanders off to check out the other rooms, and I'm left alone with Adrian.

"You too," he says. "I'd be gone if it weren't for you."

"Or because of me," I point out. "Mangus thinks I'm the reason you got caught. And honestly, his reasoning makes sense."

He brushes the comment off.

"I'm serious. You came to help me. You didn't have to do that." He wouldn't have been near the De Luca family if he hadn't been trying to get me that phone. I shudder to think what would've happened if he hadn't programmed it with Mangus's number. And it's only because he killed Fredrico that the family was shocked enough for us to break him free.

"I got caught because of me, not you," he says in a low rumble. "Stop blaming yourself."

A wave of exhaustion passes over me, and I yawn despite wanting to stay awake. My vision goes a little blurry, and I want nothing more than a bed. Looking at the dirt floor almost makes me want to cry.

"Come on, sleepyhead." He takes my hand and leads me into one of the dark rooms.

I'm slightly jealous that he doesn't have to sleep because I'd love to stay up and talk about things between us, but I'm beat. He sits down with his back to the wall and tugs me down into the dirt next to him. "Not exactly the Ritz Carlton," he teases.

"Ah, that's too rich for my blood anyway." I settle in and lay my head on his shoulder. Despite the cold, the closeness, and the hard planes of his body, I find myself relaxing and drifting off to sleep.

I wake reluctantly, teetering on the edge of falling back under.

"How are you feeling?" Adrian's raspy voice pulls me from the lapping waves of slumber.

His voice is pained, and I sit up, my eyes adjusting. There's not much light to go by, but with the added abilities from the venom, I can see everything. "I'm doing okay. What about you?"

He's still sitting in the same position he was when I fell asleep against him. Did he stay that way while I slept? Unmoving with nothing but his own thoughts?

"I owe you an apology," he says softly, and I study his face. He's serious––appearing like he hates himself, and I want to shake it away. This isn't the Adrian I'm used to. "I never should've involved you with my kind. I made that fake blood vow with you out of pure selfishness, and if I could go back I never would've done that."

I know where he's coming from, but I can't help the pang that hits my chest. Is he saying he wishes we'd never been together? Does he regret everything? My face falls, and he cups my cheeks with his hands.

"Please don't mistake me. I don't regret being with you, but I do regret hurting you. I've ruined your life."

"You haven't," I sigh, angling back to get a better look at him.

"If it weren't for me, you'd be back in New Orleans and none of this would've happened." He shakes his head, and a thick strand of golden hair topples to cover one eye. I push it back, and he winces.

"We can't speculate on what would or wouldn't have happened."

"Hugo wouldn't have targeted you."

"I'd killed his new prodigy, though," I press. "I did

that. Me. That was my choice and had nothing to do with you."

"He wouldn't have known it was you if you weren't staying with me at the Alabaster and came in bleeding that night. Think of where you are." He motions around to the dilapidated basement. "You're hiding out here because of me. I've made your life infinitely worse, and I'm so sorry."

"What about my mom?" I argue. "You compelled her to give up her addiction. She never would've gotten better if I hadn't met you."

He sighs and leans back into the wall again, staring at the ceiling. "Addiction isn't that simple, Angel. I did what I could, but who's to say she won't wake up one day and make a different choice? Find a new vice? Compulsion can only go so far."

"Well, I'm still glad you did it." Does he not understand what that means to me? What anyone with a family member struggling with addiction would give to have the same offer? I'll take all the bad with Adrian if it means I get the good sometimes too.

"I did it because I owed you. Again, purely selfish on my part."

And now I know he's lying. He never owed me that. "No, Adrian, you did that because you care about me." I take his cold hands in mine and squeeze. "Don't try to deny it. I've been angry with you for so long, but only because I didn't want to admit the truth."

His eyes snap to mine. "And what's the truth?"

"That you're my ally and my friend," I swallow hard, "and more."

"I'm going to find a way to make you safe again," he growls, leaning forward to kiss my knuckles. "I'm going to give you your life back. I swear it."

"Stop——"

"And when I do, I'm going to leave you alone."

That's not what I want. His eyes are so earnest. He means every word, but those words are killing me. This isn't what I want. I see now how bad things have been for him. He's not a "good" man, but he's not a "bad" one either. He's like everyone else, living in the middle, doing the best he can with the crappy hand he was dealt.

"I said stop." I crawl into his lap and run my hands up his arms, then up his neck to thread my fingers into his hair. I press my forehead to his. "I forgive you, but it's you who needs to forgive yourself." My voice trembles as I say what's been on my mind ever since he told me about his past back in Versailles. "And you need to forgive yourself for what happened to your wife and unborn child all those years ago."

He's completely frozen, and I can't tell if he's processing or locking down. But then his eyes are on my mouth and his lips follow, and I lose all thought. His mouth is healing me, or maybe mine is healing him, because something unlocks between us. I'm overcome with a new level of vulnerability I haven't felt with anyone before, not even him when we were back at the palace. Warmth spreads from my heart and out into my chest. So perfect. So natural. I deepen the kiss and the warmth continues to grow.

Abruptly, Adrian sets me on my butt. He's up and backed into the corner of the room before I can blink. "Eva," he whispers, but he doesn't have to say more because I see it.

My hands are glowing again.

Not just my hands. My whole body. I'm lit up from the inside out with golden light––a light that is about to kill him.

CHAPTER 31

I jump up, about to scramble from the room, when Adrian speaks, "It doesn't hurt."

I turn back, and he's staring at me with utter amazement. He takes a step forward, and light reflects off his smooth skin. I flinch back toward the door. "It's okay," he continues, "it already got me. I should be ash by now, but I'm not."

"I don't understand," I mumble. "I killed all those vampires." I look down at my hands, my arms––they're still lit up. The light emitting from them is a soft golden glow that fills the room. "This doesn't make sense."

"You could probably kill me if you wanted to, but you don't want to kill me." He steps closer still. "So maybe that's the difference."

I mull that over in my mind. "It's about intention?"

He shrugs, and a smile stretches across his face.

When it happened the first time, I'd been under

attack and the light had been a brighter white, blasting from my hands. It had come from a place of fear and desperation. But this? This is different. This is a lovely golden warmth that emerged from my heart and spread through my body when he kissed me. Adrian must be right, which means I have access to different kinds of light. Or maybe it's the same light, but I can use it in different ways. Either way, this news is revolutionary.

And dangerous.

"Nobody can know," I whisper.

He nods, and then he's back, wrapping his arms around me. "Your secrets are safe with me from now on. I promise you."

I shouldn't, but I believe him. "This doesn't hurt?" My light is wrapping around his body in a gentle caress.

"Not at all. It actually feels really nice." His voice goes hoarse. "I haven't felt this kind of warmth on my skin since I was human. I'd forgotten what it was like." He steps back and marvels at me. "You're like the sun, Angel."

He's right. That's exactly what this light reminds me of—like the golden hour when the sun is setting and the world goes fuzzy and warm. The light fades from my body as my excitement slows. It soon retreats, and I'm back to normal.

"What do you think it means?"

He stares at me for a long minute before speaking. "That you're a gift." His smile falters. "And that you're right. We can't tell anyone about this."

The rest is unspoken. Vampires have been trying to find a way to return to the daylight for centuries. This quest could be exactly why Brisa had wanted to find the fae so badly. She probably thought they could help her. What if they could use my gift to do it? My very existence could end human civilization as it is today. Everything would change.

"Do you think Mangus saw?" I whisper.

Adrian shrugs.

"Saw what?" Mangus's voice booms into our space as he opens the door. "Saw you kissing? Don't worry, I heard you making out and, no offense, but I don't need that lovey-dovey stuff right now. I went to check the perimeter. The sun set an hour ago; it's time for us to get moving."

I have no way to tell if he's lying, and I pray he isn't.

Adrian looks me up and down as if checking for any residual light, and then takes my hand and leads me from the room. We head outside, and nobody speaks. We take flight immediately, following Mangus into the darkness.

This time, I do fly myself, and it's relatively easy. It's like walking, once you get it, you get it. And I've got it. We're about ten feet up, gliding quickly over fields of green. There's no wind tonight. The outside world is quiet and peaceful, but my inner world is a jumbled mess. I don't know what's going to happen, and I'm afraid I've lost control. And now we're headed to a fae portal, which seems so unbelievable I'd laugh if I didn't know this was really happening.

It doesn't take long. We stop just outside of an ancient-looking graveyard, and I can't help but shiver. This would be beautiful if the energy here didn't give me the creeps. Everything inside is screaming for me to get away. I step back, unable to proceed.

"Are you guys sure about this?" My voice comes out strained, but I don't even care. I just want to get out of here.

"That's the wards," Mangus says. He grabs my hand so I can't run off, but I'm willing to fight him if I have to. "They've made it so that anyone who comes here will immediately want to leave, supernatural or human or otherwise, everyone gets hit with that same feeling of dread."

"That's exactly what this is," Adrian's voice shakes. "Dread."

"You have to fight it."

Mangus's words are making sense, but my intuition is still screaming at me to run. I force those feelings into the background and hold onto Mangus and Adrian. The three of us walk together into the graveyard, a line of power against the wards. I feel stronger with them at my side. They give me the inner strength I need to get through this.

We weave between moss-covered graves so old and dilapidated that the inscriptions are unreadable. It's darker here than it was outside of the graveyard, perhaps that's one of the wards as well. A fog rolls in so fast and thick that I lose most of my visibility.

"We got you," Adrian says, squeezing my hand. I squeeze back.

"This way." Mangus leads us toward what I assume is the center of the graveyard. The fog clears, inking away on an ethereal breeze, and a massive tree looms above us. Its trunk is as wide as a house with gnarled branches growing in every direction like thick outstretched arms. The tree isn't of this world. Every season is present at once––caterpillar-green leaves the size of my face on some branches, buds of pink and white on others, some are covered with crumpled leaves of every autumn color, and several bare branches glitter with winter frost.

I'm drawn to it like a moth to a flame. I can't help but want to touch it. I reach my hands out, but Mangus yanks me back. "We go together."

I blink, perplexed by the sudden need to touch the tree, a need that hasn't diminished by Mangus's outburst. Wordlessly, the three of us link arms and Mangus is the first to touch the tree's ruddy bark. The world flashes and then goes dark as we're thrust forward. I hang on for dear life and squeeze my eyes shut as my body spins. It's as if we're being thrust through time and space, or something very near to it.

We stop abruptly. I blink, taking it all in, first amazed that we're still standing and hanging onto each other, but then amazed by the new world that has materialized around us. The tree is still in front of us, but the Irish graveyard is gone. A forest of crystalline trees of pure silver and gold and a blanket of black night still overhead are in its place. Long strings of purple mist weave through the trees like ribbons. One stops at our feet and then rushes away as if it's got a mind of its own. Maybe it does.

"What was that?" Adrian asks.

"A messenger to let the guardian know we're here," Mangus says. "Now don't touch anything. And I mean *anything.* This is not our realm, and we're not meant to be here."

"Oh joy," Adrian mutters.

Truth be told, I'm still in awe even though my gut says he's right. "This is the most stunning place I've ever seen," I whisper, "it's straight out of a fairytale."

"No, Eva. This isn't a fairytale, and you're no princess," Mangus corrects. "One mistake here and you're dead, so let me do the talking."

I nod once.

"And for God's sake, whatever you do, don't eat anything."

The ground shakes. I've never experienced an earthquake before, but this is exactly what I imagine it would feel like. Adrenaline strikes through my veins and my knees weaken as I try to keep steady. Something shoots out of the ground a few paces away from us, rising up like a small mountain. The ground calms, and upon further inspection, I gasp. It's a cottage. Exactly like one you would see in a fairytale.

"Isadora is an earth fae witch," Mangus explains. "She's also a guardian of the portal, making sure people like us turn back if we do happen to make it this far."

Adrian frowns. I can tell he wants to say something, but he stays silent.

The front door to the house creaks open. "Back so soon?" A wispy voice floats from inside. "And you brought company this time."

I swallow hard.

"Please, come inside."

"We're good out here," Mangus says, shooting us a look that says do not go in that house under any circumstance.

The voice sighs. "Very well, I'll come to you." The woman is not what I'm expecting. In my mind, an old crone would step from the earthen hobble to make deals with us, but in reality, it's a gorgeous fae who glides toward us. She's petite and pointy, with a slender waist and sharp shoulders, cheekbones, and of course, pointed ears. Her white-blonde hair flows in tight curls all the way down to her knees, and her olive skin glistens with emerald green undertones. She wears a tight gown resembling moss, and as she moves closer, I realize it actually is moss that's clinging to her body. She's gorgeous and earthly and terrifying all at once, and bright amber eyes flash to me as if sensing my fear.

"We've come to strike three deals with you," Mangus says.

"One deal," Adrian quips, glaring at his brother.

"Three deals," Mangus repeats, and I'm confused. We're here to make a bargain for magic to seal the council into a blood bond and force the vampires to follow the rule of law. That's what I agreed to. And it's a great plan that will take one bargain with the fae witch, *not three.*

What is Mangus up to?

"Did you not appreciate the last bargain, vampire?" Isadora's smile spreads across her face like a sunbeam, her beauty amplifying tenfold. I don't trust it, even though it draws me in. Glancing at my companions, I suspect they're feeling the same way. Their eyes are pinned to the fae, their faces are soft, and their bodies are unnaturally relaxed.

"Your spell to release me from my maker's blood bond worked, but had unintended consequences," Mangus says darkly. "My wife was killed in the process."

Isadora pouts and traces pointy fingers along Mangus's cheek. "You poor thing. Do you need consoling?"

"Enough––" Adrian cuts in. "We're here because we need you to recreate a vampiric blood bond similar to a master and a prodigy." All eyes turn on him as he explains what's needed. It's an intricate plan, but a good one, and by the end of it, Isadora seems impressed with the ingenuity.

"I can do it." Isadora's amber eyes flash gold with mischief. "But it's going to cost you a great deal."

"Name your price," Adrian says.

She turns and grins in my direction. "I'll take the girl."

CHAPTER 32

 freeze, readying my stance. If I have to fight this woman, I will, but I don't know what kind of magic she possesses besides the earthquakes, so I doubt I'll win. The tree from the graveyard is several paces behind us, and I prepare to make a run for it. If it doesn't send me back through the portal, I don't know what I'll do.

"You're not touching her." Adrian glowers at the witch. His rage is a growing inferno, and he has no problem putting himself between me and Isadora.

"Oh, relax," Mangus drawls, "nobody is going to hurt your little angel." He smiles at Isadora. "As I was saying, there are three things I'm here to bargain for."

"Mangus––" Adrian hisses.

"There are actually two blood bonds that need addressing," Mangus continues unperturbed, "the one

Adrian described, and the one that strips Eva here from having any control over my kind."

I frown, questions spinning me to dizziness. What is he talking about? Does he mean he doesn't want me to have power from the venom anymore? But that has nothing to do with control over his kind. "I don't know what you're talking about," I say, "but I don't consent to whatever the hell it is you think you're doing, Mangus."

Both men turn on me. "So you really don't know?" Adrian asks.

"Of course she knows," Mangus snorts. "It's quite obvious."

Know what? I know that the venom has made me strong enough to survive their kind, but that's about it.

"Let's get this done. We don't need her consent for this anyway." My breath hitches, and he shoots a sly grin at the witch. "What else do you want?"

Isadora's eyes squint as she looks me over, but I'm more confused than ever. I don't understand what I'm missing. Everyone knows about the venom already, so what else could they be talking about? "I already gave my terms. I want the girl."

"I'm not for sale." I glare and step back.

"Nobody is touching Eva," Adrian agrees.

"Fine," the witch huffs. "Then I'll take the next best thing." Her bottomless eyes pin me in place. "Her blood."

I shake my head.

"Only a thimble-full. You won't miss it."

"Can't you take something else?" Adrian growls. "You can have my blood. As much as you want."

The witch hisses. "I don't want your dirty blood, vampire. I will change the blood bonds, but this is my payment. Take it or leave."

My heart thuds in my chest. I don't want to give her my blood, but I want the vampires secured under Adrian's new government. It will save countless lives.

"Let's not forget the third request." Mangus steps forward, voice growing desperate. "Bring my wife back. She was wrongly accused of my death because of your spell."

That's new information . . .

"Even if I could bring a vampire back, I wouldn't," the earth witch hisses. "Don't ask for that abomination."

"Please, I'll do anything." His eyes flash violently to me, and I'm certain he's about to offer me over, but when our gazes meet, something inside of him crumbles. Can he do it? Will he? Would I do the same if I were in his position?

"Enough," the witch's booming voice breaks through the forest like a crack of thunder. "I will spell your blood magic, but l will not perform necromancy." She points to Mangus. "And you will give this up. Even if you were to find a fae dark enough to bring your wife back, she wouldn't be the same. She'd be a shadow of herself, and she would hate you for it."

His head falls, but he nods solemnly. I feel bad for

him except for the part where he seemed mighty willing to hand my life over in exchange for Katerina's.

I turn on the vampires. "I'll do it, okay. I'll give a thimble of my blood to your witch, but I have some terms of my own."

"Don't do it." Adrian surprises me. "Let's go. We'll find another way. Your blood is not worth what--"

"Let her speak," Mangus cuts him off. "We came this far."

I take a deep breath and draw on my desire to do the right thing, even if it costs me. "I'll help with the blood bonds if you promise that you'll do everything in your power to keep me and my friends and family safe from vampires." My heart aches to think of what this will mean for my romance with Adrian. As much as I want him, I think of Mom and Felix, Ayla and Seth, and I know it's for the best if we part ways before this goes any further. "You have to promise to make sure vampires leave us alone."

They're going to make up two of the council members and have more control over their own kind than they ever before. It's the least they can do for me.

"Is that really what you want?" Adrian's throat bobs, and his eyebrows furrow.

The truth is, my head and my heart want completely different things, but this isn't about what I want anymore. This is about what I need. "Yes," I whisper.

He takes my hand, squeezes it, and then drops it. "Alright then."

"Done," Mangus promises. "You have our word."

I peer down at my shoes and then up at the witch before I lose my nerve. "Do it."

Her mouth quirks. "You know, most people wouldn't give up the kind of control you currently possess," she says, "which leads me to believe you don't know what you have."

"Control?" My mind reels. "I've never had control. Not once. Not in all my life."

"Well, you did, but it's too late now," she laughs, snatching my hand in hers so fast I almost don't see it happening. Her fingernails are long, pointed, and the same color as her mossy gown. She drags one along the top of my index finger, slicing a small incision into the skin. A crimson bead rises to the surface and she squeezes.

Part of me wants to pull away, to go back on my word, but I can't move. And it's not because I'm afraid, although I am, it's because I've become immobilized by her power. I gasp as earthy roots wrap around my arms and limbs, they move just as fast as she does.

"Almost done," she whispers, "Don't worry your pretty little head. It'll all be over soon."

"What do you want my blood for, anyway?" I whisper back, but she doesn't answer. Whatever it is, it can't be good, and maybe Adrian was right. But if doing this gets the vampires off my back and allows me to live a somewhat normal life and keep my loved ones protected, then it'll be worth any cost. "What did you mean about giving up control?" I ask instead.

This question, she does answer––an answer that guts me down my center.

"Looks like you took possession of the royal bond from Brisa," she says with a little cackle. My ears ring, and my throat itches. I can hardly believe what I'm hearing. "Your friends figured it out. Too bad they didn't tell you."

If they'd told me, everything would've been different.

"Of course, I sensed it the moment the three of you broke into my domain. And to think, you could've bossed around these princes. Ha! Wouldn't that have made you queen?"

"Stop talking, witch," Mangus growls from behind me. "You've done enough already."

And Adrian says nothing.

I try to look over at the men, but the vines hold my head in place. I can hear them, but I can't see them. The night goes eerily silent as Isadora's confession sinks into me like a knife––a blade of betrayal that I can hardly believe, but that I can't deny has sliced me clean open.

"How long?" I whisper.

She smiles. "Long enough."

It definitely wasn't a thing when I was at risk for being turned because Adrian didn't help me, so it must have solidified later. I revisit the interactions I've had with vamps over the last twenty four hours and realize they've done everything I've asked. But how was I to know? I've been running from vampires and hiding out alongside nephilim with so few opportunities to tell a vampire to do anything. Did Tate know? Did Camilla? I don't think so. If they had, they would've been much more forceful with me. Or maybe they did know, maybe that was why they were trying so adamantly to get me on their side. *No.* Because they would've made me ask Adrian about the Gateway outright, which I never did.

"Don't worry, little angel, I'll make sure they stick to their agreement with you." The witch pouts, but she's not sorry at all. Her eyes gleam with delight. "I do feel a little bad about this, you know. I'm no dark witch, I do have a heart."

I glare. "Could've fooled me."

She dramatically clasps her hands to her chest. "No really, I have a heart. Only dark fae give up their hearts for power."

She rattles on, but my mind drowns her out, the revelations spinning through my head. I had everything I needed to change the entire world, and now it's all gone.

She finishes squeezing the last of the blood into her thimble and caps it off with a lid, tucking it into the moss of her gown. I expect her to release me from the vines, but she doesn't. I'm stuck, and panic begins to bubble. I suck in quick gasps of air as my eyes fill with hot tears.

She begins to speak in a language I don't know, the consonants longer than anything I've heard before. A wash of peaceful warmth trickles through me, allowing me to relax just a little, but it's quickly replaced with an empty nothingness.

They're talking now. Somewhere behind me. They're talking. She's telling them that I have no more power over them. She's saying that the binding of the vampire council's bond is temporary until they complete her spell. She's saying that her magic only goes so far and will require some work on their part. I'm too over-whelmed to catch much of their conversation, and the harder I try, the harder it is to listen.

"Breathe," I say softly to myself. "Just breathe, Eva." This is important. Somehow I know I need to be listening in, catching every last detail.

"And when do we do the ritual?" Mangus asks.

"The next full moon." If the new moon was yester-day, then the full moon will be here in a few weeks. I want to scream at Adrian for the position I'm in, but I keep my mouth shut. It's almost like I'm forgotten by all of them, trapped in these blasted vines, facing a gold and silver forest while they chatter like I don't exist.

The gold . . .

It calls to me, a reminder of who I am and what I can do. If I can just pull my angelic light to the surface, I can get out of here. I can break free, and they'll wish they'd never underestimated me when I turn that light on them. All of them.

"You're not the only vampires to have found me," Isadora says, knocking my focus away from golden light to what she's saying instead. "But I do hope you'll be the last. We don't care for your kind here. If you fail to complete the spell, don't come back. There will be no second chances."

The vines snap away, and I fall to my hands and knees. I expect pain, but the earth is soft, as if it's caressing me. Consoling me. Is this Isadora's doing? Maybe she doesn't hate me like she hates the vampires. Maybe she really does feel sorry for me. Before I can question her, Adrian's familiar arms are lifting me, and his mouth is whispering against my ear, "Thank you."

CHAPTER 33

We leave the same way we came, hurtled through time and space, returned to our realm in the blink of an eye. The magical forest is gone, replaced by the foggy graveyard. We land next to each other among the tombstones. This time, the ground is not so forgiving. I hit it hard. It knocks the wind from my lungs and rattles my bones.

Get up, get up, get up . . .

But my body doesn't want to comply. My thoughts are a riot. My heart is numb. I'm still floating in that awful emotionless void, still stunned by everything that just happened. Adrian lifts me into his arms again, and then we're flying, up and away. The night is pitch-black, but he seems to be in a hurry anyway. I blink through watery eyes, noticing that Mangus is flying right next to us. He looks the same as I feel––utterly broken. He really must have thought he'd be able to get his wife back.

We don't go back to the old farmhouse. We fly over a city and land on the roof of one of the tallest buildings in the city's center.

Where are we? I think, but when Adrian answers, I realize I've spoken aloud. I hadn't meant to. My thoughts and my words are mixed together, and I wonder what else I've been saying during our flight here.

"We're in Dublin," he says. "The coven here are our friends. They'll house us for a day or two until we can get back home."

Back home. It doesn't seem real.

Mangus drops his face into his hands. "And where's your home?" I ask him boldly. A fire has reignited within––he'd *used* me tonight.

But Mangus turns away, and Adrian is the one to answer. "Mangus doesn't have a coven, so he's coming back to New Orleans until he figures out his next step."

So that's it then. They got what they wanted. At least I'll be able to return home, but it won't change the fact that the De Lucas will be waiting for me. Everything that happened with them still stings. It hurts that I can't trust them. My own family.

My own family . . .

Something about that rings alarm bells in my head, but then it slips away as Adrian stands me upright and I take in the glittering city lights and the beautiful Georgian-era buildings. I have no trouble with my vision, so at least I didn't lose the abilities the venom gave me.

"I haven't been here in over a hundred years," Adrian breathes. "So much has changed, and then some things look exactly as I remembered."

Mangus nods.

"But what I do remember is that the coven here is ruthless. Has that not changed? Are you sure they're our allies in this?"

"They voted for our plan," Mangus says.

They discuss their plans while I walk to the edge of the rooftop to admire the view. It's truly spectacular, and I'd give anything to be here under different circumstances. "Another bucket list item to check off," I grumble. But I won't. This doesn't count.

I hear mention of the full moon and Isadora's name, and a shiver runs down my body. What will she do with my blood? I don't know anything about fae, and I have no idea what to expect, but since they seem to stay in their realm and we stay in ours, I hope that whatever she does won't affect me here.

I swing around to say something to the men, but they're already strolling toward the rooftop doorway without me. Mangus swings the door open and Adrian walks through. I'm so startled, I almost let them go. "Hey, wait," I call. "You're just going to leave me here?"

They look back, squinting at me for a long second, and then Mangus says. "Come on then."

I step forward just as a loud crack hits the rooftop,

followed by a couple of shadowy figures falling from the sky and several more crawling over the edges of the roof. The shadows stop moving, and I realize they're not shadows, they're vampires dressed in black.

"We've been looking for you," Sebastian says with a sharp-toothed grin, his focus zeroing in on me. His trenchcoat swooshes around his ankles as he takes a step closer and my nerves turn to ice. They're surrounding me on all sides, more vampires than I can comprehend, and far more than I can fight.

I call upon my light magic, willing it to the surface, but nothing happens. I glance at my hands, shaking them out.

Someone tackles me to the ground, and my hands are quickly tied behind my back. I don't understand the different kinds of light yet, but the one I'd killed Brisa with had sprung from my hands. It was nothing like the golden all-over light I'd conjured from kissing Adrian. My face is pressed into the hard surface of the rooftop as someone sits on top of me, keeping my hands restrained and my body pinned tight. The ligaments of my shoulders burn, and I muffle a cry.

"What do you want?" I crane my neck up. Where is Adrian? Mangus? Surely, they'll stop this. But then I see they've also been restrained, and even though they're impossibly strong, there's an entire coven's worth of suckers here to keep them in line.

"You betrayed me," Mangus growls at one of the Irish-looking vampires, but the burly man only shrugs and says that had he known about me, he would've sided with Sebastian.

So what do they know about me then?

Sebastian kneels down to get a better look at me. Is this it? Is this the end of my life? So many times I'd told myself I'd rather die than become one of them, but now faced with death, I'm not sure I'm that brave. It's all too much, and I almost beg him to turn me.

No. I won't do that. I'll never do that.

"Stand her up, Kenton," Sebastian motions to the fanger with their knee currently jammed into my spinal cord. "I want a better look at her."

My heart races. "Kenton?" I gasp as the man hauls me up. I crane my neck back, and sure enough, it's my old friend holding my arms.

I'm reminded of the first time I met him. It was in that graveyard and he'd handed me the stake that had ended up saving my life. "You were dead," my voice cracks. "I saw you. You were dead."

His eyes flash to me, red-rimmed and glowing with bloodlust. "Oh, I remember, Eva. How could I forget dying for you?"

Guilt wracks my chest because he's right. He died in battle for my life. Or at least, I thought he'd died. He must have still been alive, clinging onto the last shreds of life, and then one of them found him.

"She brought me back," he explains, his voice a low rumble against my ear. "And she made me so much stronger."

"I'm so sorry," I whisper. The tears break through and leak down my face. I'd give anything to go back and save him from this fate.

"Don't be," he sneers, shoving me toward Sebastian.

Sebastian's grin is ruthless when he grabs hold of me. He looks so much like his twin, Hugo, that I'm momentarily speechless. "Tell her," he nods to Kenton. "What is life like as a vampire? Is it really as bad as you believed it to be?"

I stare at my friend as his old familiar smile lights his face and then fangs slip out of his gums. "Being a vampire is incredible," Kenton steps forward, and his harsh voice softens. "When it's your turn, you're going to love it. I promise."

"When it's my turn?" I squeak. He sounds so much like the old, caring Kenton. My stomach twists. This was his worst nightmare.

"Don't worry," Sebastian says. "That won't happen for a long time, and when it does, you'll be begging for it."

"Wait, who is 'she'?" I question my old friend. "Who found you?"

Kenton's smile is genuine, and my heart drops for the boy I loved deeply. The boy who fought alongside me for all that is supposed to be good and right in the world. "I'm one of the princes now," he says. "Isn't it wonderful?"

"I––I don't understand."

His eyes glitter with possibility. "Brisa is my maker."

"That's a lie," Adrian growls from over Sebastian's shoulder. "Brisa is dead."

"We felt the bond break," Mangus adds. "Sebastian, you did too. Don't lie to these people." He looks around at the coven of vampires. "Well, are you going to just sit here and let him lie to you?"

"Did you feel the bond break, though?" Sebastian asks his brothers. "Or did you feel the bond transfer? Because you see, it turns out there's a big difference."

That's when the truth of it hits me.

I took Brisa's royal blood bond, but I didn't actually kill her. And it's not as if I saw her die. Nobody did. There was light and there was screaming and then there was nothing.

The crowd of shadows parts, and the vampire queen steps through, her glowing amber eyes right on me. She's as beautiful as ever, and radiant in her rage. "Hello, Evangeline," she says, "I believe you have something that belongs to me."

"Actually, she doesn't. There is no more royal blood bond." Adrian pushes his captors off him with the force of a hurricane and strides right up to Brisa. He's a man possessed by revenge and without an ounce of fear. The way he is toward her now is a complete one-eighty to how he was with her before.

Brisa's eyes go dark. A breeze catches her honey hair on the wind, and it whips behind her as she snarls. "You dare to betray me? Oh, I know all about your pathetic council."

Adrian's laugh is maniacal. I've never seen him like this. "Betray you? We thought you were dead. How can I betray a ghost?"

"You didn't even try to find me! I went into hiding and was right to assume Sebastian is the only one of my children left who is worth anything, considering your and Mangus's disgusting behavior."

"What would you have had us do?" Adrian throws up his hands. "Try to have three princes rule together without a royal blood bond to make sure our laws are actually imposed? We'd have been assassinated." He points to Sebastian. "By your *oh-so-worthy* son."

"It doesn't matter now," she says in a clipped tone, "I'm back. And I will forgive you if you help me, but if you get in my way, I will kill you." They stare off, neither willing to break. Mangus drops his head.

No. This can't be. Things can't go back to the way they were.

"She was always going to kill you," I burst out. "She told me." I look at the three brothers. "All of you. She said she was going to start a new line of heirs, starting with me."

The men don't react at all. Had they known, or is this news? Brisa turns those killer eyes on me, strides forward, and slaps me clean across the face, her sharp nails cutting the skin. It burns hot, but I refuse to back down. "You would be wise to keep that mouth shut. Have you forgotten with whom you're speaking? I am the queen of all vampires."

"Not anymore," I hiss back. "There's no royal blood bond, remember?"

Her pupils dilate as long, thin fangs extend. "With or without the blood bond, I am still queen. I'm taking the bond back, and then we shall see what becomes of you after we are through with your gift."

I swallow hard. Of course, she wants my gift. She saw it, she survived it. And now she wants to do something with it. And when she's done, there's no doubt she'll kill me. The hatred burning through her eyes is great and terrible––and directed entirely at me. But strangely, I'm not afraid. A sense of calm takes control of my body, and everything becomes crystal clear.

"And how exactly are you going to take it back?" I tilt my head, looking her up and down. She needs me, which means she needs me alive.

"It transferred with our exchange of blood the first time," she says, "so we'll exchange blood again to transfer it back."

Except that it's gone, done away by fae magic. I open my mouth to argue, but she's too fast. Like a bullet leaving its chamber, she's on me, sinking her teeth deep into my neck. I scream out as pain slices through me and venom pours into my veins. "Last time you did this I almost killed you," I say between gasping breaths. "How can you be so sure it will work this time?"

But my hands are bound, and everything feels different than before. Worse. I start to fade. She's drinking so much so fast. My knees go weak. Then Brisa is being ripped away from me, Adrian the one pulling her off.

"There is no more royal bond!" he booms, and the world goes silent. "You're going to kill the only asset you have left."

The only asset she has left . . . I fall to my knees, trying to breathe, trying to stop my heart from breaking at his words. Everyone turns to look at him, half the group curious and half the group gearing to rip his head off.

"We didn't know you were alive," he says carefully, "so we took Eva to the Gateway."

Brisa's eyes go wide, and Mangus laughs from where he's being held by the door. "Why did you think we came to Ireland, Mother?" he calls out. "Wow, you've really lost your edge, haven't you?"

"What did you do?" she growls, and Mangus is thrown at her feet. "What did you do!"

"You killed Katerina," he glares up at her. "You blamed her for deaths that were your own doing. All the princes? Is Eva telling the truth, *Mother*? Were you killing off your children one by one only to pin the blame on Kat?"

She glares right back. "I did as I saw fit. Those who are weak are culled. This is our way, don't act so surprised."

He rolls onto his back and laughs. "So she admits it, ladies and gentlemen."

"What did you do, Mangus?" She drags him to standing. "What happened at the Gateway?"

He spits in her face, and she rears back, horrified.

"Guess what, mommy-dearest? I don't have to tell you shit anymore."

They're about to fight, and it's one Mangus won't win, but he doesn't seem to care. I do, though, and I care about Adrian and Kenton who might get caught up in the fray.

"They made a bargain with a fae witch!" I yell.

"Eva, don't," Adrian growls.

It doesn't stop me. "The effects of your precious royal blood bond have been transferred to the vampiric council." Satisfaction sweeps through me as the crowd murmurs, and Brisa's face falls. "So yeah, I don't have it anymore. I never even knew I did, or believe me, most of you bloodsuckers would be dead by now."

Brisa screams––and maybe I shouldn't have added that last part. Sebastian goes for Adrian, and Mangus is jumped by several vampires at once just as Brisa dives for me. I'm on the ground in an instant, my head pounding against the stone. I'm going to die. There's no doubt in my mind that she intends to kill me. I'm no use to anyone now, and I'm a liability to the vampires if I'm alive. But at least I beat her in this one thing.

"Leave me alone," I cry when her fangs catch my neck again. She'll tear me apart in seconds. "Stop! Leave me alone! All of you, please––" the last part is a choked sob.

She's there, uncaring, violent––and then she's gone.

I blink and sit up, trying to catch my breath. Inexplicably, they're all being dragged away as if by some invisible force. *What in the world?* I don't understand it. I reach out toward Adrian, trying to catch his hand as it reaches toward me. His eyes are panicked as he yells, "This is the condition you made. It's the fae magic!"

And then they're being pushed off the rooftop and are lost to the darkness.

Every last one of them.

I jump up and run to the edge of the building, searching the streets below, but there's no sign of them. It's just a quiet, beautiful city in the middle of the night. Not a soul to be seen--not even the soulless.

I press my hands to my neck. It's slick with blood. I've already lost a lot, and my mind is hazy and light. My fingers search out the wounds, but I find that they're already knitted back together. There's so much powerful venom in my blood now that I healed as quickly as a vampire would have.

But I'm in no danger of becoming a vampire because I didn't take any blood from her tonight. We didn't get that far. No locking myself up for three nights.

I blink, the realization of Adrian's final words hitting me--it was the fae magic. I yelled at Brisa to leave, demanded they all go, and they did. Not by choice, they were forced away, as if by magic.

The fae said that she'd make the vampires hold up their end of the deal with me, and boy did she honor that. She got a thimble of my blood, they got their spell for the council blood bond, and I got my wish, that the vampires would leave me and my friends and family alone.

And when I demanded it, all of them were forced away.

I want to cry, to scream, to laugh, to smile, to rage . . .

but I do none of those things. Instead, I walk to the edge of the building and jump, levitating down to the street without issues. I need to get out of here. Not just out of Dublin, but out of Ireland.

It's time to go home.

CHAPTER 35

Turns out fleeing a foreign country without any money or identification is no walk in the park. I wander around the streets for a few hours attempting to come up with a plan. I'm shivering and have no clue where I am, and I'm not as smart as I thought I was because I've literally got nothing. When the sun finally rises, I feel as if I can breathe fully again. The light bathes the city in warmth and calms my nerves.

I sit down on a bench and close my eyes. *You can figure this out.*

It's not like when I was in Paris and had a countdown clock hanging over my head. At least now the vampires can't come after me. The nephilim are another story, but they won't know where I am, and by the time I get back to New Orleans, I'll have come up with a better plan to avoid them, even if it means getting Mom and going on the run. Adrian made sure my rent was paid and had worked out a deal with Pops so I can return to my old life, but I know that's not in the cards anymore. Mom and I will have to go start a new life somewhere else. We can get new talismans to take with us.

It seems too simple and too impossible all at once, but it's the only plan I've got, so I cling to it. First things first, I need safe passage out of Ireland. I frown down at my tattered clothing. I'm in all black, which helps hide the blood, but I'm also filthy and need to find something presentable to wear. I'll have to convince someone to let me use their shower and give me new clothes or access to a washing machine. While they're at it, some food and water would be nice, but I'm not going to count on that.

The thought makes my stomach grumble. What do vampires do when they're in situations like these? Oh, that's right, they just compel humans to get whatever they need. I obviously can't do that, but I'm as fast and as quiet as a vamp. Maybe I can sneak into someone's flat while they're at work, and then once I've gotten myself cleaned up, I can find the U.S. Embassy. This is the capital of Ireland, so there should be one, and if anyone can help me get back home, they're my best bet.

I find an apartment building that doesn't look nice enough to have good security and peer up at the windows. The sun reflects off of them, so I have to go around the corner to look from a different angle. I feel icky, but I don't know what else to do. Most of the windows are covered with curtains or blinds, but a few aren't, and I can see right into several living rooms.

A car screeches to a stop right in front of me. I slink back against the brick building just as a door is thrown open. My immediate instinct is to run, and that instinct is confirmed when Leslie Tate glares up at me as he climbs from the vehicle. He's quickly followed by Camilla and the twins, Enzo and Nicco. The twins are fast, splitting to either side of me, boxing me in.

"How did you find me?" My fingers clench, and I glance up. I could fly, but we're in broad daylight and there are people around. Right now though, I'm not sure that will stop me.

"A lot of people care about you, Eva," Tate says. "We're here to help."

Another door opens and a rumpled-looking Felix and Seth climb out. I gape at them, wanting to tell them off, but they shoot me sharp warning looks that make the hairs on the back of my neck stand. Something isn't right, and now isn't the time or place to interrogate my friends. I just hope they hadn't gone running back to the nephilim. I don't think I can take another betrayal.

"They didn't know I was coming to Ireland," I challenge. "So why don't you tell me how you really found me."

Camilla smiles and smooths out her already perfect

silver hair. "You're a smart girl. Think on it for a while, and it'll come to you."

I have thought about this––how Tate knew to find me outside the catacombs and how he's conveniently known about some of the vampire's whereabouts. Even back in New Orleans, he came to Adrian's suite when I was locked up there, not to retrieve me but to do something else, something I still haven't figured out.

"Well, I know your boys here are trackers," I nod to the twins, "but that doesn't fully explain how you keep finding me, especially back in Paris. If I had to guess, I'd say you have a mole somewhere in the vampire's organization."

"Ah, very good," Camilla winks. I know she won't outright give up her source, but I'm dying to know who it could be. All the vampires I've met seem pretty keen on staying alive, so an alliance with the neph doesn't make sense.

"Why can't you let them go home?" I point to my friends. "They're good people with bright futures that you're ruining."

"How many times do we have to tell you, Eva?" Felix pipes up. "We want to be here. We want to hunt and protect. School and everything else can wait." I'm not sure he believes the rhetoric he's spewing. How can I know if that's the real him or the one manipulated by Tate's mind-tricks?

I'm preparing to make a run for it when Camilla pounces. For an old lady, she's fast as a whip, grabbing hold of me and hanging on tight. I scream and push her away, but then Tate is on me too, holding me still while his mother-in-law slides into my mind. Her attack is violent and thorough, riffling through memories and ripping them to shreds in the process. It burns like an instant headache, and I gasp in horror.

Just when I think I'll pass out, she releases me, and I stumble to my knees. I glare up at her through strands of dirty hair, hoping she can see the vitriol in my eyes. "You are a murderer," I seethe. "I know what you did to my father––to your own child. You make me sick."

She stomps her foot, and I jump. "You don't know the whole story."

"I know enough."

"Sacrifices have to be made. This is a war. And we'll continue to make sacrifices to win it."

My eyes flick to my friends, and I know this is a veiled threat. She'll kill them if I don't cooperate. For the first time, I'm pretty sure they know it, too.

"Get in the car or see what further sacrifices I'm willing to make," she demands.

I have no choice but to get in, I'm not going to risk my friends. They slide in after me, and I buckle up. I'm exhausted and angry, but most of all I'm frustrated. I feel so hopeless. There's nothing I can do. Getting away from the De Lucas the first time was hard enough, but now Camilla knows everything. She knows I can levitate, she knows about the blood bond, she saw me go to the Gateway. She has *everything*.

"I'm not happy about the blood bond," Camilla says. "I can't believe we missed that."

"Sorry to disappoint," I snort.

"And that blood you gave to the fae," she continues, exasperated. "Do you know what you've done? Do you know what a fae can do with a nephilim's blood freely given like that? They can't just take it, they have to have it given, and you barely put up a fight."

I scoff, "But you saw exactly why . . ."

"To help the vampires," she lifts a brow. "Oh, I saw enough."

I fold my arms over my chest and glare out the window. It's not like she's going to answer my questions about the fae anyway. And what does she expect here? I did the best I could in a crappy situation.

"But I do have to thank you for something marvelous you did on your little adventure."

I turn back. The car is one of those limousines that seat a bunch of people, and they're all staring at me now. "And what's that?"

"You're smarter than I gave you credit for."

"What did she do?" Tate asks.

"The fae cast a spell, and Eva made sure the spell included something valuable." My throat goes dry, but I let her finish. "The vampires are not to hurt her friends and family. Isn't that sweet?" She taps her fingers together in excitement. "And they're to leave them alone."

I roll my eyes. This isn't her business.

Tate and Camilla smirk as if they've just won the lottery but can't let anyone know until they've secured a good lawyer.

"What?" I give in, curiosity getting the best of me.

"You already know," Camilla taunts.

"I don't――"

And then it hits me . . . *family*. At the time I'd been thinking of Mom's well-being, but she's not the only family I have. The De Lucas are my family too. I've unwittingly made it so vampires can't harm them.

"Congratulations," Tate deadpans. "You figured it out."

I sink back into my seat, the gravity of the situation dropping a million pounds of weight onto me. I can't believe I was so foolish. If the De Lucas can't be harmed, then they'll be free to hunt vampires as they see fit. Months ago it would have been great news, but I feel differently now. I still hate most vampires, but they're not all bad, and I have friends who are vampires now. Mangus helped me, I'm still in love with Adrian, and Kenton got a second chance.

"We'll start with the princes." Camilla turns from me to direct orders to Tate. "Take them out, and then we'll work our way down the ranks."

I shake my head. "No!"

"Hush, girl. Let the grown-ups talk."

"Adrian and Mangus aren't bad. They're not the ones you want."

That does it. All the De Lucas glare daggers at me as

Tate sneers, "Believe me, they're the ones I want to kill first, especially Adrian. And how can you say he's not bad when you saw him murder Fredrico?"

Were we not in the same room? They were torturing Adrian when he did that. They're the ones who forced it out of him, they're the ones who put Fredrico in that position to begin with. But they don't care, they've got an opportunity to strike at the vampires, and they're going to seize it.

"Wait," I interrupt, heart hammering in my ribcage. "Brisa is still alive. Camilla saw that, too. Take her out first. She's the worst of all of them."

"She's powerless now," Camilla grins wickedly, "thanks to you, my dear." She studies me for a long minute, and I don't know what to say. For once I'm completely speechless and out of ideas. There's nothing I can do. I don't even know who my enemies are anymore because everything has gotten so convoluted. I've made a mess of it all, but the one thing I know for sure is I don't want Adrian,Kenton, and Mangus to die. Not even for a bigger cause. Not even if it's the "right" thing to do.

"You can be a team player or you can be locked up," Camilla offers. "Your choice."

What choice is that?

"I'm a team player," I lie because being locked up isn't going to help anyone. I have no intention of hurting the vampire princes unless we're talking about Sebastian, but if I can be part of the team to hunt them down, then maybe I can warn them before it's too late.

"Good." Her eyes flick to Felix and Seth, and I know the threat is there again. Do what she wants, or watch the ones I love pay the price. "First things first, take us to the Gateway."

My mouth pops open. The last place I want to go is back to that fae portal, and I certainly don't want to see the witch again. She even said she didn't want us to return. I can't go back there. "Why?" my voice cracks, and I swallow my fear.

"Because we've been looking for it, and you can get us there," Tate states the obvious while simultaneously avoiding my question, but Camilla can tell I'm not satisfied with his answer. She sighs heavily.

"As long as there are abominations walking this earth, then it is our duty to see them destroyed," she says. "It's why we've been placed here. It's what we're meant to do." She leans forward and pins me with her dark crinkled eyes. "It's what you were made for. Stop denying who you are, embrace your destiny, and watch as your gifts flourish."

Embrace my destiny? One where I kill anything that isn't nephilim or human? One where I feed off of human energy?

No, I can't. I won't. Not ever.

But I'm smart enough to nod my head and tell her exactly what she wants to hear. "You're right. I'll take you to the Gateway."

"You're doing the right thing," Tate says.

But I'm not. I know that. No matter what I choose, someone is going to be hurt. There are no clear choices, no right or wrong answers. The world is not black and white. It's gray. It's a series of maybes and what-ifs and trying to stay alive. And I'm no better than the rest of them because here I am playing along, joining in their games.

I can't be better than them, I've tried to take the moral high ground so many times and failed to the point of making things so much worse. I have to accept it.

I'm not better than vampires.

I'm not better than the other nephilim.

Or the fae.

Or *anyone*.

I've wanted to believe I was, but the truth is I'm not, and the only way I'm going to beat them is if I play on their level. I remember enough to direct the De Lucas in the general direction of the Gateway. Once we find the graveyard, the rest will be easy. In the meantime, I make a conscious decision to embrace my dark side.

I'm tired of playing by a set of rules that are constantly changing. It's impossible to win, and I'm done. Maybe I wasn't meant to be the hero of my story. Maybe I was meant to be the villain. In storybooks, the good guys always prosper, the light always trumps the darkness, and the impossible odds win out. But this isn't a storybook. This is a real-life war, one that has spanned for centuries and claimed millions of lives. I refuse to be another casualty, not notable enough to mention by name. Just another statistic. Another failure. Another sad story forgotten by time.

If you can't beat them, join them--and make them suffer.

*

Thank you for reading! Continue on for character art, information about the next book in the series, and more about the author.

Felix

A LETTER FROM NINA

Thanks again for reading. I can't do this without you and I hope you enjoyed this book! I'd love it if you'd be willing to leave a quick written review on Amazon and Goodreads. If you haven't joined my amazing reader group yet, I'd love to have you there as well. You'll get access to novellas and deleted scenes, plus you'll be among the first to learn about new projects. The Facebook group is called Nina's Reading Party. I also offer signed copies in my Etsy shop, Nina Walker Books. And hey, please continue to the next page for the next cover reveal. The PREORDER is up, please note I'll publish as soon as I'm able!

Happy Reading,

Nina Walker

NINA WALKER

GOOD THINGS COME
TO THOSE WHO STAKE

TRUE DEATH

VAMPIRES & VICES, NO. 4

The Color Alchemist Series

    1 - Prism

    2 - Fracture

    3 - Blackout

    4 - Collide

    Among Shadows - Prequel Novella

    The Official Color Alchemist Coloring Book

Bleeding Realms - Dragon Blessed

    1 - Crown of Dragons

    2 - Kingdom of Spirits

    3 - Throne of Embers

    Ashes Fall - Prequel Novella

Vampire & Vices

    1 - Blood Casino

    2 - Cruel Stakes

3 - Wicked Sun

4 - True Death

New World Shifters

1 - Night of the Wolf Moon

2 - Lies of the Blood Moon

3 - Rise of the Wild Moon

4 - Fall of the Harvest Moon

Standalone Novels

Dark Ocean Princess

Twinfluence (by Grace Costello)

Ivy League Liars (by Grace Costello)

AND SO MUCH MORE TO COME!

ACKNOWLEDGMENTS

If you read the dedication, this book is for those brave souls battling chronic illness. I've joined those ranks over the years, but while writing this series things got pretty bad for me. I'm okay--I've learned a lot and I'm slowly healing, but I really just have to take the time to say thank you to my readers who have been so patient about book releases and so understanding about the challenges I've faced being a creative person with physical limitations. Thank you so much.

I also have to thank Ailene Kubricky for editing, Kalynne Art for character art, Yocla Designs for the series covers, my friends and family for continued support, and my awesome proofreading team and enthusiastic ARC team.

Love you all!

ABOUT THE AUTHOR

Nina Walker writes YA paranormal romance, urban fantasy, dystopian fantasy and more. *Wicked Sun* is her 16th book. She lives in Southern Utah with her sweetheart, 2 kids, and 3 pets. She loves to spend as much time outdoors exploring the real world as she does exploring other authors' brilliant imaginations. You can also find her romantic comedies under the pen name Grace Costello.

www.ninawalkerbooks.com

Facebook Reader Group "Nina's Reading Party"

Instagram @NinaBelievesInMagic

TikTok is @ninawalker.books